"These aren't kids' games we're playing now . . ."

"Brad, don't," Terry protested, "you're hurting me."

But his grip only tightened; slowly he began to pull her toward him. He wrapped her in his arms and crushed her against his chest. "And even kids get a goodnight kiss. . . ."

With a small moan, Terry let her mouth open and pressed her body against his, letting herself glory in the feeling of his muscular legs, his insistent loins pushing against her own. Then Brad raised his head, whispered her name and kissed her hard on the lips . . .

Dear Reader,

Your enthusiastic reception of SECOND CHANCE AT LOVE has inspired all of us who work on this special romance line and we thank you.

Now there are *six* brand new, exciting SECOND CHANCE AT LOVE romances for you each month. We've doubled the number of love stories in our line because so many readers like you asked us to. So, you see, your opinions, your ideas, what you think, really count! Feel free to drop me a note to let me know your reactions to our stories.

Again, thanks for so warmly welcoming SECOND CHANCE AT LOVE and, please, *do* let me hear from *you*!

With every good wish,

Carolyn Nichols

Carolyn Nichols
SECOND CHANCE AT LOVE
The Berkley/Jove Publishing Group
200 Madison Avenue
New York, New York 10016

HEARTLAND

LYNN FAIRFAX

HEARTLAND

Distributed by Berkley/Jove

First edition published March 1982

Printed in the United States of America

Second Chance at Love books are published by
The Berkley/Jove Publishing Group,
200 Madison Avenue, New York, NY 10016

HEARTLAND

chapter *1*

DESPITE THE GLOWING reviews, despite the crowds that jammed the little gallery, despite press requests for private viewings—despite *everything*—Terry Rovik, a native Chicagoan, absolutely *refused* to go any higher than cloud *eight!* She hadn't waited this long and worked this hard to be flustered by the surprising overnight success of the first one-woman showing of her painstakingly crafted nature photographs.

Terry Rovik was a blonde, a stunningly beautiful blonde. But she wasn't a dizzy one. In fact, Millie and all her other good friends thought she was one of the most sensible people they had ever met.

Stepping into the posh downtown hotel's crowded elevator, Terry turned to face forward, a demure, almost enigmatic smile momentarily playing across the finely planed features of her strikingly attractive, porcelain-pale, faintly Slavic face. As the glass-walled elevator crawled slowly up the inside of the hotel's spectacular atrium, Terry stared straight ahead, ignoring both the frank admiration of the tuxedoed men and the envious glances of the formally gowned and bejewelled women surrounding her.

After all, what did they have to fear from her? Wasn't she too sensible and business-like to be flirtatious, especially tonight? And couldn't they see that this was no social affair she was on her way to, even if it was in the hotel's swanky rooftop restaurant? Her black crushed-velour blazer, matching skirt and shoes, and white blouse, not to mention her attitude, should have told them *that,* she thought.

She recalled the unanimous praise of the Chicago papers: "... a real respect for the thing in front of her," one said, and "... print after print records the decisive moment," ballyhooed another. Terry wondered if the reviewers knew they were paraphrasing the two most influential photographers of the entire twentieth century. And now here she was, on her way to a dinner meeting with the husband-and-wife New York publishers of renowned fine art books.

From sometime art and biology student at the university and part-time clerk at a local photography store to perhaps soon-to-be famous photographer and author in just one short week: it was *almost* enough to take anyone's breath away!

Terry fought hard to bring her soaring hopes and fantasies under control. She used an old photographer's trick. Looking out over the impressive multistory interior lobby of the new hotel, she emptied her mind of thoughts and speculations and made a mental catalogue of everything that she saw. All around her were curved balconies, dripping with potted ivy and flowering bougainvillaea; directly across from her, an indoor waterfall dropped seven stories to a pool in the center of the lobby; bracketing the clear, marble-bottomed pool, escalators descended to the parking levels below.

Here was a group of Japanese tourists; there, a young couple on their way to a school prom . . .

Terry smiled. Those days were long past for her; even her days as a full-time college student at the university were now more than seven years behind. Of course they had been good times, but she wouldn't exchange them for *this*. Taking a quiet, deep breath, she resumed her mental descriptions of the people below:

Here was a gregarious Texan in a Western suit and cowboy hat; there, an elderly couple, holding hands, out for a rare night on the town. Here, striding briskly across the lobby to the down escalator . . .

No, it couldn't be! Terry stared hard after the already disappearing, foreshortened figure: *Was it?* She hadn't seen him for seven long years, except on television of course, and now there he was, a figure glimpsed at a distance.

An electric shiver—like the feather-light touch of his hand—ran down her spine, and she had to fight back the urge to turn and run after him. Her heart beat rapidly and she closed her eyes and concentrated to control her breathing. Of course it could be him, she told herself.

Hadn't she just seen him on that popular news-magazine TV show of his, getting his two colleagues' congratulations on some award or other? And hadn't Brad—who, his dark good looks notwithstanding, was the fair-haired boy of television journalism—announced that he was taking a leave of absence, his first long vacation in many years? Didn't it make sense that he would come back to his native Chicago for part of that vacation? And didn't it also make sense that he would stay here, in the newest, fanciest hotel in town?

Terry shook her head in amazement at the workings of fate. One minute sooner and she would have run right into him; a minute later and she wouldn't have known that they were even in the same state.

As the elevator doors opened on the restaurant's fifty-story-high night vista, Terry took a final deep breath and strode briskly out, not a trace on her face of the emotions and the shock that had swept through her only moments before.

"McMasters party," she said, and the obsequious maître d' immediately led her to a well-situated little table along the glass outer wall, with a magnificent view.

The dark, slowly revolving restaurant took twenty minutes to make a complete circuit. From the Loop to the lake shore, like a giant constellation, the twinkling lights of all of Chicago seemed to rotate below her.

Now, as the great obelisk of the Sears tower hove into view for the second time, dinner was silently cleared away and replaced with coffee and brandy, and the small talk was coming to an end.

"We just love Chicago, don't we, Caroll?" Sarah McMasters asked her husband. A tall, angular, aging businesswoman, her wiry black hair was streaked with gray. She put another of the long brown cigarettes she had been chainsmoking into an elegant onyx and gold holder and placed it in her scarlet lipstick-lined mouth. Expertly, she flicked on her small gold lighter. The momentary, harsh flame revealed sagging, lined features under her make-up; the light was reflected from her pinprick brown eyes that, even as she squinted from behind the cloud of thick smoke, watched Terry with almost predatory concentration.

"Yes, we certainly do," agreed her balding, bow-tied, endomorphic husband Caroll, once again playing Mutt to her Jeff. It was a practiced role, Terry could see. "That's why we were so glad to come here to make the final arrangements for the next edition of our Going Home Again series," he continued enthusiastically.

Sarah cut back in smoothly. "Are you familiar with it, dear?" she asked, blowing out a thin, compressed stream of smoke.

Terry took another small sip of the Chablis she was still nursing before she answered. So *this* was what they wanted her for, she thought, realizing at the same time that they had never used a photographer in this prestigious series. "Indeed," she began, carefully placing the delicate crystal goblet back on the table. She was glad that her friend and agent Millie had briefed her so well. "Those books are quite well-known. I believe I've seen write-ups on them in *Time*, *Art World*, the Sunday supplement. Didn't the last one win a special national book prize?"

"For art excellence," Caroll noted proudly.

"Yes, of course," Terry continued, "and deservedly so. That was the book by the author they always compare to Steinbeck, about his trip back home to northern California. The paintings that illustrated it *were* lovely," she said with genuine feeling. "Tell me, are all the books in the series like that? I mean, do you always get a famous author to return to where he was raised, or to where he writes about, and do you always match him with a famous painter who does the illustrations? Quite frankly, I think it's a brilliant idea."

"Thank you, dear. We had no idea it would be such a success," Sarah replied in her slightly rheumy voice. She put down her brandy snifter and picked up the cigarette. "That is what we've done in all six books. But we're thinking of some changes for the seventh."

"Oh?" Terry interjected innocently.

Sarah took another drag on her cigarette. "Yesterday we just happened to step into that charming little gallery where you're exhibiting," she said casually, "and we fell in love with your lovely, evocative pictures, dear. We think they might fit into our next project. . . ."

"Really?" Terry showed mild surprise. "Why, thank you. What project was it that you had in mind?"

"Well, our latest author assures us that all over the Midwest, within a short flight from Chicago in every direction, are to be found places of great natural beauty and variety, the kinds of places where our author often traveled with his family as a young boy and to which he still often returns."

"Yes, it's true," Terry agreed softly, slipping easily into her naturalist's vocabulary, "there are many such natural habitats and ecological communities—unspoiled places of great charm and, as you say, 'variety.' Sometimes I think that they're the best kept secret of this part of the country."

"I could just tell from your pictures that you'd feel that way, too," Caroll piped in eagerly. "It's *that* feeling we want to capture in the book. It's one of the reasons we plan to call it *Travels Through the Heartland,* or maybe just *This Heartland*. Do you like it?"

"Yes, that's very good," Terry replied. "Yes, heartland."

Leaning forward, Caroll pressed on. "At first, we thought we were going to get another fine painter. We had in mind David Hoc—" Sarah's scarlet-tipped warning hand on his arm stopped him immediately. "Oh dear," he mumbled under his breath.

Terry knew that he was about to name a West Coast impressionist, world famous for his delicate watercolors, which were often compared to those of such masters of the form as Turner and Constable. His price, Terry also knew, would be ten times what the McMasters could get her for. She smiled. "I'm flattered that you would think of me," she told the momentarily abashed Caroll.

Again Sarah cut in. "Yes, dear, we do hope we can work out all the arrangements with your agent so you can join our project." She waved her cigarette holder imperiously in Terry's general direction. "What gorgeous looks, don't you agree, Caroll? With that lovely hair like spun gold and those chiseled cheekbones, you should be on the other side of the camera, my dear," she observed pointedly.

"Thank you," Terry said simply, with an almost demure graciousness she did not *entirely* feel. After all, this was an observation she had heard more than once—it seemed as if everyone from the clerk at the corner grocery ("You oughta be in pick-chas, lady.") to her art-department faculty advisor ("Young woman, perhaps you'd care to earn a little extra money modeling for me on Saturdays?") judged her by her appearance *first*. And what if she returned the favor to Sarah McMasters? What would someone who looked like an old harpy say then?

What she *did* say next was rather surprising. Sarah drummed her fingernails on the table, took another puff from her cigarette, leaned forward and in a quiet, confidential voice said, "Dear, I just know we're going to be able to work this project out. Quite frankly, you're perfect for us, and we're all aware of what a good opportunity this is for you; so, for all practical purposes, only the details remain to be settled. Is that agreed?"

"I suppose," Terry replied warily.

"Now then, dear, I'd like to speak to you a moment not as a publisher, but as a mother. . . ."

Her husband looked surprised. "Sarah, don't you think it would be better . . ."

She waved him off. "No, I'd prefer to have this out in the open," she said firmly.

"You see, dear," she continued, "I'm quite aware that *Travels Through the Heartland* will require that our author and you, a *most* attractive young woman, must spend quite a bit of time alone together, out in nature, in what we can easily suppose would be, shall we say, 'romantic circumstance'."

Terry realized her cheeks were burning, and not just with embarrassment. "How 'thoughtful' of you to be so 'concerned' for your author's 'welfare,'" she observed with undisguised sarcasm. "If you feel a chaperone is necessary . . ."

Sarah backtracked immediately. "No, no, no. I have no doubts about your motives. I do trust you *and* our young man, and a chaperone would be *entirely* out of place. Please don't misunderstand me. I do value you as an artist, and I'm hopeful that this book will be the first of many ventures for us. . . ."

Terry was mollified. She didn't need a reminder of all the good these two could do for her. "You did say you were speaking as a mother. Son or son-in-law?" she asked with a pleasant smile.

Sarah smiled back. "Soon-to-be son-in law. When our daughter, our *only* daughter, Caroline returns from a trip abroad, they'll set the date. But for now it's all a big secret."

Terry found Sarah's concern both very human and quite touching. "I do see," she said. "Let me assure you with as much candor as you've expressed that I've *no* romantic interest in *any* man, and I intend to keep it that way. I've had some experience with those entanglements, and, believe me, *never* again. It's just not worth the pain.

"And the thought of knotting up my professional affairs with an affair of the heart is just totally abhorrent. How could I conceive of such a thing, when it would cause grief to you, the very people who are showing such faith in my work and my photographs? I'll even promise, on my word of honor, that if your son-in-law-to-be, for whatever reasons, does *anything* that could be interpreted as an advance, *I* will discourage it."

Sarah received Terry's declaration with a wide smile. "You do promise it?"

Terry repeated solemnly, "Yes, I most certainly do."

Leaning back in her chair, Sarah sighed with relief. "I knew I could count on you, dear," she said expansively, "and I do hope you won't take anything I just said personally. I'm just such a worrier, and you're so attractive and dear Brad is such a catch. . . ."

"Brad?" Terry's eyes narrowed. Her breath caught in her throat. "You don't mean . . ."

"Bradford Andrews, the TV journalist," Sarah continued. "Do you know of him?"

"I, uh, I thought I saw him in the lobby earlier—from a distance," Terry mumbled in mounting confusion. She took in a shivering breath. "I, uh, watch his show sometimes."

"Who doesn't?" Sarah responded obliviously. "Frankly, that's just why we decided to broaden the Going Home series to include more than just authors; after all, not many people read anymore, but *everyone* watches TV. We've already done the market research and we think that Brad's book is going to be our biggest seller yet. He was such a dear to offer us the idea and sacrifice part of his vacation. Actually, it isn't such a sacrifice, really, because his hobby, as you may know, is botany and geology. He's quite the amateur naturalist, just as you are. Personally, I find it all rather tiresome—no offense—it's just that I'm a city girl, New York born and bred and . . ."

Never had such complex emotions assailed Terry:

was it possible, she wondered in that corner of her mind that was still observing and thinking rationally, for a person's heart to leap for joy and sink with dread at the same time? Hers certainly seemed to be doing both.

It seemed incredible that her past and her future should collide like this. Across the table from her, Sarah was still talking, chattering happily now that the deal was all but made and the promise had been given, but Terry didn't hear a word of what she was saying. In her ears was a roaring; around her, the lights of the city seemed to spin.

Caroll was giving her a peculiar look. "Are you all right, Miss Rovik?" he asked solicitously. "You look so pale."

"I'm fine . . . thank you," Terry managed to say, in a voice so calm that it surprised even her. "It's just the wine—I'm not used to drinking, you see—and the height and the lights of the city. . . ."

"There, there, we quite understand," Sarah said tolerantly. "All this excitement. It's been quite a long day for us too. Now if you'll just say whether or not you can, we'll just call it an evening and I'll have our secretary send the contract to your agent as soon as we get back to New York."

"If I can? . . ."

"Begin next weekend, of course. As I said, even with Brad using his own plane he'll be on a tight schedule, so once you begin you'll be traveling almost constantly. . . ."

"Yes, of course. I quite understand," Terry said in a level voice that didn't betray her. She realized it was time to decide. Life was always like this, she thought, there was never enough time or information for the really big decisions; you just trusted your instincts and hoped for the best. "I'd be honored to participate, that is, if Mr. Andrews will work with me—an unknown—then yes, of course I will," she said, shocking that part of herself that wanted to just tell them—to be done with *him* once and for all—and to leave.

Sarah was all delighted smiles. "Oh, don't worry about a thing, dear. We'll work everything out. Just leave the details to us and your agent."

"Then if you'll excuse me," Terry interjected, trying not to be abrupt, but knowing she couldn't take much more. She realized she would blurt the truth out if she stayed one more second. "I'm quite tired, I'm afraid, so I'll just say goodnight and thank you again." She stood up and shook hands with both McMasterses, declining Caroll's offer to see her to the elevator, and somehow managed to walk back across the dark, crowded restaurant.

As she turned the corner Terry heard Caroll say to his wife, "Funny, isn't it, that this charmingly modest young woman would say the same thing about collaborating with Brad that he said about her?"

Sarah, lighting another cigarette, asked without much interest, "What's that?"

"When her name came up before, didn't Brad say, 'I'll do it if she'll work with me'?"

Sarah shrugged. "So?"

"Just odd," Caroll observed. In the mirrored wall next to the elevators, Terry could see him signaling to the waiter for the check.

chapter 2

TERRY HAD BEEN thinking about this morning all week. What would their first meeting be like?

While she rode the el from her gabled Oak Park rooming house into town, to visit the little art gallery where her photos were still on display, visions of the scene to come flashed across her mind as rapidly as the fragments of townscape vistas—factories and freeways, playgrounds and parking lots, house after rundown house—flashed by the windows of the speeding train.

While she waited in a grocery line, or sat in one of her graduate art classes, or went to her part-time job at the local photo-supply store, she imagined what their first meeting might be like. She had every intention of keeping her promise, but there was an unavoidable rose-tinted hue to these musings about her reunion with the World Famous Journalist.

Later in the week, as the morning approached, during the interminable procedures required to withdraw from her classes, and after the arrangements were made to quit her boring job (What a relief to be free of the drudgery, no matter what the reason!), she reexamined her motivations and the events of the dinner with the McMasterses, going over them time after time.

Could she really go through with it? she wondered. Would she really be able to keep her promise to Sarah now that she knew the man was Brad? Surely, she still didn't feel the same way toward him that she once had! And, surely, he didn't feel *anything* for her! Then why did her body thrill at the memories? Why did her body remember when her mind so desperately wanted to forget?

Now here she was in the airy living room of her small attic apartment, packing her cameras and lenses in her battered tan camera bag and her clothes in a matching suitcase, talking about all of it with the only person in the world to whom she had confided the whole story, Millie Foster. Not only had Millie been her landlady for the past five years, she was also her good friend and the person who had such faith in her that she had taken Terry's photos—on her own initiative—to the gallery, thereby becoming her *de facto* agent.

"You should've seen me run out of there," Terry recalled with a smile, as she carefully packed away the wide-angle 55 mm f/4.5 and the 250 mm f/6.3

telephoto lenses for her Mamiya C330 twin-lens reflex camera. She was wearing loose-fitting, pleated walking shorts of brown twill, matching knee socks, ankle-high hiking boots, and a brown, long sleeve crew-neck shirt; purposely dressing down, wearing clothes appropriate to the job of tramping through the forest, rather than trying to create a favorable first impression. "It's amazing that the waiters weren't trampled."

Millie laughed, a deep, hearty sound that shook her dimpled cheeks and her ample bosom. "No, you did exactly right," she observed. "The McMasterses were *mighty* impressed with you. That Sarah called me the next day about the itinerary and to say the contract was in the mail. 'What a *dear* person, *so* professional,'" Millie mocked, doing a wicked imitation of Sarah McMasters' affected pronunciation.

Terry smiled at her friend. "Yes, the itinerary," she repeated with a frown.

"Do you know it? Are you all set?"

"Do I know it? It's burned into my memory. I knew most of it long before the McMasterses called. You know, if *I* were planning this book, those would be *exactly* the places I'd choose."

Terry paused thoughtfully, putting the last of her clothes into the suitcase and shutting it and the camera bag. It had been years, but she *had* been to every one of the places on the McMasterses' list: the woodlands in rural Illinois, the wildlife sanctuary on the Michigan lake shore, the peaceful, slow-moving Minnesota river, the secluded, shimmering lake in the midst of a vast prairie. "Do you think Sarah suspects?" she asked.

"No way," Millie said emphatically. "From what

you said about that little dinner, if she even had an *inkling* you wouldn't be going anywhere *near* the airport and this Bradford dreamboat of yours." She glanced down at the watch on her freckled wrist. "Speaking of the airport, we'd better get going. We don't want to be late."

"You're sure you don't mind driving me all the way out there?"

"Honey, I wouldn't miss getting a glimpse of TV journalism's Mr. Heartthrob for the world. Let's go."

Of course they got hopelessly lost. Brad's plane was in a distant corner of the vast airfield, to which neither Millie nor Terry had ever before had reason to go, and it took them forever to find it. In fact, by the time Millie had negotiated, in her battered Chevy, the maze of back roads leading to the appointed gate, they were more than half an hour late. Strangely, Terry remained calm, but Millie was frantic.

"Oh no, I'm so sorry. How could this happen? The letter said *promptly* at ten. Something about flight plans and air traffic. Oh, gracious, I think we're there!" She jerked the car to a stop, raising a cloud of dust. "It's him," she whispered, pointing with her chin, her hands still tightly gripping the wheel.

It *was* him, striding purposefully toward the car. He was wearing cowboy boots, tight jeans, a light cashmere V-neck sweater without a shirt, and a crinkled leather jacket with a fur collar, just the kind that the heroic young flyers in all the World War I movies wore.

"I didn't know he was so tall," Millie whispered.

"Thanks for everything," Terry replied, kissing her

nervous friend on the cheek. She stepped out of the car, took a deep breath, and faced him.

"Hello, Brad," she said softly, praying that her knees wouldn't buckle and that he didn't hear the quiver in her voice.

"Hello . . . Terry," he replied in that deep voice familiar to millions, and known to her from more than just the TV. He dipped his head toward her, as if to kiss her cheek, and then pulled back, a strange, almost anxious, look flickering across his craggy face; *this* was something that his viewers had never seen, not even in the heat-of-battle reporting which had first made him famous. He cleared his throat. "You're late," he said gruffly. "We've got to get going."

"I'm sorry, Brad. We got lost," Terry replied, barely aware of anything but the nearness of his presence.

"That's okay," he muttered, looking away from her. He peered into the back seat of the Chevy. "Those your bags?" he asked.

"Yes."

Brad pulled the door open and leaned into the back seat to get the two bags.

"My friend Millie," Terry said from behind him. "I'd like to introduce you to her. Brad Andrews, Millie Foster . . ."

"I watch you every week," Millie gushed.

"Thank you," Brad replied quickly, in a tone that cut her off like a knife. "My pleasure." He turned away without looking at her, a bag in each hand. "Let's go," he said, striding away without looking back to see if Terry was following.

Terry felt Brad's rudeness to her friend like cold

water dashed on her own face, and on her feverish sensibilities.

She sighed. *This* wasn't what she expected at all. She reached into the car through the front window and picked up her white cableknit cardigan sweater, exchanging a rueful look with the crestfallen Millie.

"Don't worry," Terry joked, "I'll get you an autograph."

Her friend gave her a sympathetic little smile. "Mr. Andrews goes to war," she said sardonically.

Terry laughed in spite of herself. "Thanks again, Millie. Now don't get lost going back. Bye." She threw the sweater jauntily over one shoulder and marched through the gate toward the small twin-engine airplane. Brad was already in the pilot's seat, putting on earphones, throwing switches, revving up the engine; in general, busily being the same old commanding Bradford Andrews that she remembered so well.

As she got into the plane, Terry said to herself that keeping her promise to Sarah McMasters was going to be easier *by far* than she had ever thought.

chapter 3

TERRY LISTENED ALERTLY to the hum of the Beechcraft's twin engines and the faint hiss of the wind outside. Looking out the windows at the brilliant blue sky dotted with puffy white clouds, she relaxed for the first time all morning. She was careful not to stare at Brad, who was still preoccupied with thc complex business of navigation.

The silver airplane was a small but powerful six-seater. Until it had left the city far behind and they were flying southwest, high over the rich, rolling farm country that bordered the Illinois River, Brad's attention was focused completely on the bank of instruments before him. Now, as they sailed through the clear spring morning, he flipped on the autopilot and pulled off his headset.

Then he unfastened his seat belt, got up, and leaned over Terry, who was still strapped into the copilot's chair. Suddenly taking her chin in one strong hand, he kissed her—hard and full on the lips.

For just a fraction of a second, Terry's mouth responded greedily, wantonly, as if it had a life of its own. A part of her wanted to close her eyes and swoon, to press against his mouth with her own forever. But instead, she pulled back and slapped Brad's face.

"My, my," he said sardonically, rubbing his chin. "I see you're as hot as ever. . . ."

Was he referring to her temper or to the fire that he still could kindle deep within her soul? Terry wondered. She could feel the flush on her cheeks and could hear the little catch in her breath.

"What was that supposed to be?" she asked belligerently, to cover her mounting confusion.

"Can't a fellow say hello to an old friend?" Brad retorted.

"Aren't you supposed to be flying the plane?" Terry countered.

"The autopilot's doing that," he said, flashing one of his famous smiles. Again, he began to move toward her.

Terry lifted her hand. "Don't you dare," she warned.

"Oh, come on," Brad taunted, grinning. "Admit it wasn't so bad; admit you liked it."

"Get back in your seat," Terry replied adamantly. She wasn't ready to admit any such thing—not even to herself.

Still smiling, Brad complied with her demand and returned to the pilot's chair.

"Whew, that Chicago air traffic is always hard work," he muttered after a few moments, shifting in his seat and stretching his muscular torso. He rubbed the back of his neck with one hand, turned to Terry, and smiled warmly. "What some guys will go through just to be alone with a pretty lady," he joked, giving her an affectionate look.

Terry remembered the elaborate schemes they used to invent to be able to be alone all those years ago and she smiled back. "You could have tried the phone first," she joked, thinking of all the times when she would find Brad waiting patiently for her on the front steps of her dormitory.

Terry knew she did not dare let herself remember all their past happiness. She pushed it out of her mind. Fate had thrown them together for a brief time. Like most men Brad only wanted a fling—for old times sake. . . . But, he was engaged! She made a solemn promise to Sarah McMasters and she intended to keep it!

"But then you never were one to take the easy way, were you?" Terry added thoughtfully.

"Not the original Man of Action," Brad replied, his deep voice rich with irony and self-satire. "At least I got into the right business," he added with a sigh, his flippant tone unable to disguise his genuine weariness.

"Speaking of business . . ." Terry prompted.

"Must we? So soon?"

"That's what *I'm* here for," she said sternly. "Business *first,"* she amended, noting his crestfallen look, "then *maybe* we'll have time to talk about the past and catch up on our lives. . . .

"Besides," Terry added with a mischievous twinkle

in her eye, "I've been living a rather dull, conventional life, and I know all about what *you've* been up to anyway. A person can't go into a grocery store without having to look at headlines about Bradford Andrews's 'latest exploit' or see your 'distinguished features' on the cover of some magazine."

"Okay, okay," he conceded, "I guess I deserve that—especially for the way I acted toward your friend back at the airport.

"I'm sorry. It's just that you were so late and I was kind of nervous. . . ."

"You, nervous? The man who faced ten rampaging elephants?" Terry asked incredulously.

Brad's prominent jaw muscles twitched. He lowered his dark, flashing eyes. "With you it's different. We go back too far, and we meant too much to each other once. I always used to get tongue-tied around you." He looked up, directly into her eyes. "But we never used to have trouble communicating . . . in other ways," he added, so hotly that Terry flushed a deep red in spite of herself.

Brad laughed, breaking the momentary spell of his own intensity. "I can't fool you with my TV voice or inquiring-reporter posture, and I shouldn't even try. I'll just get in trouble every time I do. Like with my mother," he continued. "We go back too far and she knows me too well to be impressed with my, shall we say, 'recent success.'"

Terry pursed her lips. "Your mother," she repeated flatly. "How are your parents, Brad?"

"They moved from the Drive back to New York years ago. . . . Mother often asks about you."

"Me?" Terry was more than a little surprised. "The

Toast of Lake Shore Drive inquiring about Theresa Rovik, the poor little waif from the wrong part of town?" she asked acerbically. "My word!"

"Really, Terry, it's true." Brad leaned toward her, his eyebrows knitted together intently. "Sometimes I think she regrets what happened, what she did to us, more than anything she's done in her lifetime. She's had a lot of years to think about it, and see the effect it's had on me. Believe me, she's changed a lot.... So have I."

Brad stuck out his jaw in that characteristic gesture that Terry remembered and thoughtfully rubbed the deep dimple in his chin. "All right, we'll play it your way, Miss Rovik," he said briskly. "Business first ... for now."

And those last two words, holding warning and promise, made a tingling excitement race through Terry's body.

Brad sat back, faced forward in his pilot's chair, switched off the autopilot and resumed control of the airplane. "It's a short hop anyway and we're almost there. Here's the procedure," he added, tapping a dial in front of him until a stuck fuel indicator jumped from nearly empty to just past the center of the gauge. "I'll set this little bird down at a private field just below Pekin. They're expecting us there and will have a jeep and all the necessary permits waiting for us. From there, it's only twenty minutes or so into Timberline. Once we get into the preserve, it's up to us: you take your pictures, I'll make notes for my narrative. We can wander around until the light's gone for photography or until we get hungry. I know a great little country inn down there. After that, it's either back to Chicago or stay down here for the night. The little country inn has rooms and I booked one, just in case."

"Booked *one?*" Terry asked pointedly.

Brad looked over at her and grinned sardonically. "Don't worry, Miss Rovik," he said with good-humored, exaggerated deference. "Your honor is of utmost concern. Actually, I booked *two* rooms. They're very nice, *adjoining* rooms," he added significantly, with another grin, as he took hold of the stick with both hands and banked the little silver airplane, sending it into a long, slow, descending glide toward the airfield somewhere far below.

When they landed at the small, sleepy private airport just before noon, their jeep was waiting for them. While Brad spoke to the disheveled mechanic in grease-covered overalls about refueling and maintenance, Terry walked over to the one-story, cinderblock structure that served as the airport terminal to sign the necessary rent-a-car forms and pick up the keys and park permits. The rental agent—a teenaged beauty in tight white shorts and an even tighter T-shirt—was beside herself with excitement.

"Is that *really* Brad Andrews from TV?" she gushed, standing on tiptoe and straining to see out the window. "Gee, I watch him at home *all the time,*" she continued. "Do you suppose he's here on a story, on one of his exposés? I wonder if he gives out autographs. . . ." Without waiting for an answer, the excited girl grabbed a pen and a small pad of paper and started for the door.

"Hey, what about our jeep?" Terry called out after

her. "The keys, the park permits. Don't I have to fill out a form?"

"Sure!" she exclaimed over her shoulder, as she threw open the door. "Just fill out one of the forms on the counter and leave it for me. The jeep's around back. Key's in the ignition, permits are in the glove compartment." And with that, she was gone. Terry watched with some amusement as the girl pranced across the tarmac, pen and paper in hand. Brad was still talking to the mechanic near the plane's fuselage, and the girl approached him with as much wary deference and nervousness as the youngest groupie might show the most mythic rock star.

Terry continued to watch as Brad took the pen and paper and scribbled his name. When he favored his young fan with one of his famous smiles, the girl looked as if she were about to faint—or at the very least fall to the ground at his booted feet. Terry noticed the scowl the young mechanic had on his face and the obsessive way he rubbed his grease-covered hands with a grimy rag, and it was obvious to her how the mechanic felt about the young girl and what he thought of the way she was throwing herself at this big-city stranger.

Terry shook her head in bemused wonderment, then got busy with the rental forms. Afterward, she made her way around to the back of the building and found their jeep.

She got in, turned on the motor, shifted into gear and drove out to the plane. Brad and the young girl were still talking; rather, she was doing all the talking while Brad, a tolerant expression on his face, was listening patiently. The mechanic, still looking like he could spit nails, was at work on the plane's underbelly.

"Ahem," Terry said as she pulled up. She drummed her fingers on the steering wheel.

"Right," Brad replied quickly, adding to his young admirer, "Sorry, Miss Towne, we have to go. Now you just write to the personnel office, in care of the network. Feel free to tell them I said to send you out all the applications." Brad brought their few pieces of luggage from the plane and threw them into the back of the jeep. "Don't forget to have a look at that flap," he called over to the mechanic, who just nodded sullenly and waved back. "Bye now, Miss Towne," Brad said with a jaunty wave. He hopped into the seat next to Terry, who put the jeep into gear and shot off down the road just a little faster and more abruptly than she had to. They were off at last, heading south down a two-lane country road, toward the Timberline Wildlife Refuge.

Terry willed herself to concentrate on the prospects of pristine Nature ahead of her and *not* on the memories of the unspoiled past time that it evoked.

At the park entrance it was her turn. For all the handsome young park ranger seemed to notice, Brad might as well have been back in his New York office, or broadcasting from the moon. The ranger, in full uniform and a Smokey-the-Bear hat, only had eyes for Terry.

He merely glanced at their permits. "You'll have to leave your vehicle at the turnoff, about a mile and a half down the road, and hike in after that, ma'am," he said, handing the permits back to Brad without once taking his eyes off Terry's face. He touched the brim of his hat in a small, respectful salute. "I do hope you have an enjoyable afternoon, and if there's anything I can do—"

"We'll be sure and let you know," Brad cut in abruptly.

"Why, thank you." Terry smiled at the ranger. "Bye now." And she drove off, down the rough one-lane road he had indicated.

"Bye now," Brad repeated mockingly. "I'm surprised he didn't throw himself in front of the car."

Terry laughed with pleasure. "Why, Bradford Andrews, what's this? Jealousy? A double standard? At least *I* didn't sign any autographs. *I* didn't practically invite some innocent young thing to come visit me in the big city."

"I did no such thing."

"Then what was that 'feel free to use my name with the network' line all about?"

"That's different," Brad insisted.

"Different?" she repeated skeptically.

"If you're a public person like me," Brad explained somewhat defensively, "especially a newsperson who comes into people's homes asking to be trusted, you have to take the time and make the effort to be civil to your viewers. I know everybody in the business doesn't feel that way, but I do. If you don't do it, you're asking for trouble, you're asking for some sort of a nasty incident. You see?"

Terry was dubious. "What about Millie?" she asked.

"I told you I was sorry about that," Brad replied curtly. "I told you why it happened."

"Nervousness," Terry noted sarcastically.

"Stop the car!" Without warning Brad gripped the

steering wheel with one hand. To keep from swerving into one of the white oaks that lined the dirt road, Terry hit the brakes hard. The jeep swerved to a stop.

Brad reached over and switched off the ignition.

"What's the matter?" Terry asked in a worried voice.

"Shh! Listen!" he ordered.

"What? I don't hear anything," she whispered back.

"Listen harder," he replied. "Look around."

Terry took a deep breath. A soft, sibilant breeze rustled through the huge oaks and maples all around her and played across her face. On both sides of the road, the hilly, mossy forest ground was abloom with wild flowers; dogwood and blue phlox, trillium and wild geranium carpeted the earth.

"Here, now, in the midst of all this," Brad said softly, respectfully, "we shouldn't snipe at each other. I'll do whatever you want to make it up to your friend. Just let's not argue, okay?"

Terry thought it over. "Okay, Brad, you're right," she conceded. "If I'm not paying attention to all this natural splendor, I'm not going to get any good photos for the book. I'm sorry, too. Let's start all over again, from the beginning."

"Friends?" Brad asked.

"Of course," Terry said, starting the jeep up again and continuing down the road. "Friends who are doing a project together."

"So it's *still* business first?"

"Sure," Terry said, pulling into the parking area where they had to leave the jeep behind. "What else?"

Brad didn't say anything; he simply hopped out and began to unload their packs.

As they prepared to take one of the many narrow trails leading off into the woods, Terry couldn't resist asking teasingly, "Aren't you just a little bit worried about that mechanic back at the airport? He's obviously the teenager's boyfriend and he sure didn't like all that adoration she was showing you. Aren't you just a little concerned that he might sabotage the plane?"

"Not at all," Brad replied, striding into the lead. He shot her a wry grin over his broad shoulder. "Well . . . maybe I better double-check when we get back. . . ."

Terry hid behind an oak at the edge of the sun-splattered glade overgrown with blooming thistles that were crowned by flowers of pink and purple. While she pulled the little Leica with the fast-pan film out of her pack and got ready to shoot, Brad, who was sitting against the trunk of another oak tree ten feet behind her, got out his expensive Sony cassette recorder and began to record some more notes for his narrative:

"Timberline is nearly a thousand acres of marsh and forest that spreads out from both banks of the Illinois River and is home to a wide variety of wildlife," he intoned. "Although it is no longer part of the chain of Mark Twain National Wildlife Refuges, it is still administered by the U.S. Forest Service for the protection of the wild habitat.

"Geese, canvasback ducks, and colonies of great blue heron are just a few of the species of birds to be found here. Sometimes the sky is dark with flights of migrating birds. . . .

"Hey, Terry," he called out happily, turning off

the machine, "remember when we came here during the Fall that first year: mallards, wood ducks, snow geese by the thousands honking their way South . . ."

She smiled back at him. Of course she remembered: she was a freshman with her first camera, he was a senior with his book of field notes. . . . As they wandered hand-in-hand through the virgin woods and wind-swept marshes, under slate gray skies, breathing the sharp, crystal-clear air of approaching winter, it had felt like they were the first people in the world. . . .

Now she was glad to have the excuse of picture-taking to stay at a "proper" distance from this man—her first love—whom she feared still could attract her like a magnet if she didn't resist his charms with all her might.

Terry cupped the camera in both hands, took a deep breath for steadiness, and stepped out from behind the cover of the tree.

Click! She shot without focusing, trusting to instinct: the ruby-throated hummingbird was exactly where she hoped it would be, its long, needle-pointed beak sucking the rich nectar from the thistle flowers. For a moment it hovered motionless, its tiny wings beating the air faster than the eye could follow.

Just before it disappeared, Terry stopped down the shutter speed without looking and shot again. Click! Ordinarily a shot like this required a tripod, she knew, but her hands were steady and the result would be worth the risk of the lost film; if she was lucky, she would have a stop-action shot of the hummingbird, the beating of its wings frozen in midflight by the magic of the camera, perhaps even a moist, golden drop of nectar quivering at the tip of its bill.

With a satisfied smile on her face, Terry picked up her bag and walked to where Brad was still sitting. She recognized that admiring look on his face and knew that while she had been preoccupied with the hummingbird he had been engaged in bird-watching of quite a different sort.

She sat down next to him on the warm, spongy ground and leaned back against the rough bark of the tree, tilting her head back so that the mild Spring sun played on her face. "I think I just got a great shot," she said with pleasure. "I know that photos of hummingbirds are probably a dime a dozen by now. But this one is going to be different, something special. You should have seen the way the light played on its wings. There was a rainbow effect almost; it was just lovely. . . ."

"Lovely," Brad repeated quietly, "I'm sure."

In the silence that followed, Terry listened to the bird songs all around them and the sonorous buzzing of the myriad insects. "Lovely," Brad had said, and she knew from the tone of his voice that he wasn't talking about the weather or the composition of one of her photographs. "Lovely"—the word was like an invitation, like a long-closed door opening. . . .

"I've just about got all the shots I wanted," Terry said quietly, hoping to dissipate the electricity she felt building between them. Now that she was sitting down, she felt the exertions of the long day for the first time. She was glad that their path had taken them in a long, looping semicircle around a peaceful little lake and that now they were relatively close to where they had left the jeep several hours before. "Let's see, there's the landscape of the lake, with the nice fringe of trees and the clouds mirrored in the water. I like the feeling in that one. And the tree knocked over by lightning; that one's for the texture. And the ring-tailed deer . . ."

"Terry, *do* you remember the first time we were here?" Brad sat up and leaned toward her, his craggy features just inches from her face, his presence suddenly as overpoweringly elemental as any of the earth scents all around them. "Do you remember how we vowed to come back some day? It's as if fate kept us apart, kept us from here, for all those years, but now here we are. . . ."

"And I think we'd better get going." Terry stood up quickly—too quickly—and for a fraction of an instant felt as if she might swoon. She put out a hand to steady herself against the tree.

Immediately Brad was up. "Are you okay?" he asked, the concern obvious in his voice. He reached out to help her, but Terry shook her head and stepped back, away from his outstretched hand.

"I'm—I'm fine," she said, shaking her head. She shivered despite the warmth of the Spring afternoon. "I—I just got up a little too fast is all."

He handed Terry her cableknit sweater, which she put on wordlessly. She picked up her pack and held it in front of her, as if she needed a physical object as a barrier between their two bodies. "It's been a long day," she said, unable to keep a faint tremor from her voice. "It's getting late. We should get back before—before something happens that we'll both regret."

"All right," Brad agreed quietly, the note of concern still in his voice. "You look awfully pale. We both could use some dinner. Here, let me." He reached over and took her pack, slinging it over one of his broad shoulders before Terry could object. He picked up his own pack and put it across his other shoulder. "You're sure you're okay?" he asked. "You could wait here and rest. I could go and get somebody to help bring you out—I'm sure your friend the forest ranger would be only too glad to come and give us a hand."

Terry smiled gamely. "No, everything's okay now. It was just a feeling that lasted a moment. Now the moment's passed.

"Dinner sounds like a good idea. Let's head back to civilization," she added, starting off on the path that led back to the jeep. Suddenly, all she wanted to do was get away from the little glade.

As she walked briskly ahead of him, Terry was acutely aware of Brad's presence just a few paces behind her; all her senses seemed to be tuned to an exquisite, almost delirious pitch of heightened awareness. She could hear each slightly labored breath that he took, and the snapping of little twigs beneath his boots sounded like rifle shots in her ears. Her own breathing seemed shallow and ragged too, and all around her the bird songs and forest sounds rose to a crescendo....

No! she insisted to herself, balling her hands into fists and jamming them into the pockets of her sweater as she walked, *This is impossible! I refuse to let this happen to me again!*

Without realizing it, Terry had increased her pace and lengthened her stride, so that now she was nearly running down the wooded path. Behind her, straining under the load of the two packs, Brad called out for her to wait—"What's your hurry?" he yelled—but she didn't hear him; neither did she pay the slightest attention to the vernal splendors around them.

All she knew was that she had to get out of this place, and stay away from this man's overwhelming physicalness, until these sensations subsided.

He doesn't love me, she reminded herself angrily, *it's all just some game! Just business; simply fate.*

The past is gone, she repeated to herself with each emphatic footfall, *the past is dead....*

When Brad finally caught up to her, Terry was already sitting primly in the passenger seat of the jeep, hands resting demurely in her lap. She was staring straight ahead, and the only signs of her exertions were her flushed cheeks and the slightly heaving breaths that still forced their way from her breast.

"Are you all right?" he asked, a note of puzzled concern in his deep voice. He threw their packs into the back and got behind the wheel.

"Fine, Brad," Terry replied coldly, without turning her head. "It's been a long day and I could use some food and a little rest."

"Sure, but—"

"Don't say anything more," she cautioned him. "Please don't ask. Let's just hurry up and get going."

The worried look never left his face, but without another word Brad turned on the motor. He slipped the jeep into gear and accelerated smoothly down the dirt road. They rode back in an intense silence.

They stopped at the rural airfield on their way into town so that Brad could check the sullen young mechanic's maintenance work. Neither the mechanic nor his sexy, celebrity-worshipping girlfriend were anywhere in sight, and the little terminal was practically deserted.

After the long day, which was far from over yet, Terry felt exhausted. She curled up in an uncomfortable red plastic chair while Brad looked over the airplane. Then against her better judgment, for she usually didn't touch "junk food," she nibbled on a candy bar and an American cheese sandwich that tasted like cardboard. It had probably been sitting in the food-dispensing machine for six months at least, she thought, until Brad brought it and the orange drink she washed it down with over to her.

"It's just to keep up our strength until we eat a good meal," he said, but by the time they had split the sandwich and each eaten a candy bar, and Brad had confirmed that the Beechcraft was indeed ready to fly, neither one of them was hungry anymore. So they got two cups of bitter-tasting coffee from another dispenser, talked it over in a corner of the deserted terminal, and decided to fly on to Minneapolis that very night.

"This way we'll start out right in Minnesota in the morning," Brad explained. "If we make that our next stop, we'll have an easier day tomorrow. We'll just have a short drive to the St. Croix instead of spending most of tomorrow in the air."

Terry agreed to this sensible plan. And she also agreed when Brad decided to radio ahead and book two rooms at a hotel near the Minneapolis airport.

"McMasters Publishing is paying all our expenses anyway. Besides, this hotel has a nice little restaurant that stays open late," he noted reasonably, as they got into the airplane. "We can check in, freshen up, have a light late-night supper and still get plenty of rest before starting out again early in the morning."

"Okay," Terry agreed dreamily, as the plane taxied down the country airfield's single runway, raced past recently planted grain fields, and took off into the setting sun. "We can always come back to the Iowa and Nebraska stops later in the week," she added, yawning. "If we're lucky, we'll get a warm spell; that's when those places are the most photogenic anyway."

"Right." Brad pulled back the control wheel and banked toward the right.

Before the plane had ascended to its cruising altitude, Terry was asleep, rocked by the hum of the engines and the gentle motions of the Beechcraft as it flew in an almost direct line northwest, toward the distant city. She didn't awaken again until they had touched down at the busy, bustling, neon-lighted Minneapolis airport.

Then she woke to find her head on Brad's shoulder and his face just inches from hers. His strong hand was gently brushing an errant strand of her flaxen hair away from her face. "Wake up," he whispered, "we're here."

Terry batted her eyes rapidly to blink the sleep from them. She sat bolt upright. "Where?" she asked thickly.

"In the Land of Ten Thousand Lakes," Brad replied with a smile. "On the tarmac at the Minneapolis airport. It's almost ten at night. C'mon, someone's waiting for us."

Terry took the hand he offered and let him lead her out of the plane and help her down to the ground. It was the bracing northern air of Minnesota that snapped her wide awake and *not*—she told herself emphatically—the powerful touch of his hands at her waist as he lowered her to the ground, or his warmth and the familiarity of his scent as he held her, on tiptoe, against his chest for just a fraction of a second before releasing her and turning to the nervous young man who was waiting for them.

"Welcome to Minneapolis," the young man said, doffing his chauffeur's cap to reveal a shock of unruly brown hair. He opened the rear door of a long, black Cadillac limousine. "My name's Rick, sir. I'm with WACE, that's the 'ace' network affiliate out here. Mr. Moorhouse, our general manager, said I'm to report to you for as long as you need me and the car. He said it's not often we get someone so important from network visiting our little town, and it's a great honor to do anything we can to help. It's my pleasure too, sir. I've admired your work for a long time."

Brad cleared his throat. "Why, thank you," he said modestly. "This is Miss Rovik. She'll be working with me."

"Hello," Terry said pleasantly.

She could see that the young man was so abashed at being in the presence of the Great Journalist that he could do no more than nod and barely glance at the Great Journalist's beautiful consort and mumble, "Ma'am." Rick quickly scurried over to the airplane and brought their luggage to the limousine, while Brad and Terry got into the car's spacious back seat.

"So this is what you meant by radioing ahead to

make hotel arrangements," Terry observed somewhat disapprovingly.

"I had no idea they would go to this length," Brad whispered back, looking around to make sure that Rick wouldn't overhear and be offended. "I just wanted them to book rooms for us—the standard courtesy for visiting firemen, that's all."

"Well you're certainly getting the Big Chief treatment," Terry replied, giggling in spite of herself.

The young chauffeur sprinted around to the front of the car and hopped into the driver's seat.

"The hotel, sir?" he asked obsequiously.

Brad turned to Terry and whispered into her ear. "Might as well take advantage of the natives' generosity," adding, "Yes, the hotel, please" to Rick.

"By the way," Brad said to the still nervous man, after he had deposited them at their hotel and brought in their luggage, which the desk clerk ordered whisked up to their rooms immediately, "we'll be starting out tomorrow around eight in the morning. Tomorrow will be the only day that we'll be needing your services, then we'll be pushing on. Tell Mr. Moorhouse that I appreciate these kindnesses he's showing us, but officially I'm on vacation, so please have him send a bill for your time and services to me, in care of the network. That way there won't be any misunderstandings."

"Yes, *sir,*" young Rick replied, "will do." And from the admiring way he said it, Terry could tell that Brad's scruples about the station manager's offer of "free" limousine service had impressed the young man more than ever. The gesture wasn't lost on her either.

"You can't be too careful," Brad said gruffly, as they walked across the lobby to the elevators after checking in. "In this job people are always wanting to give you something, but it's never 'free,' so it's best never to accept. I just sign autographs, say 'no thank you,' and keep smiling. Believe me, it's not nearly as glamorous as it sounds."

Terry wanted to believe him—he had said it in such a heartfelt, world-weary way. She also wanted to ask him how he fit into his code this business of flying all around the Heartland and checking into adjoining hotel rooms with her, when he was engaged to his publisher's daughter. But just then she spotted in the center of the lobby, a young couple in formal evening wear, who had stopped dead in their tracks and were looking at them.

The attractive, dark-haired young woman patted her tuxedoed escort on the arm. Then she gathered up the hem of her long black evening dress in one hand and, holding her little beaded purse high in the other hand, came running across the lobby straight toward their elevator. She squeezed inside just before the door closed. As the door shut, Terry got a last glimpse of the young woman's escort, who was still standing in the center of the lobby, a disbelieving, fuming look on his face.

Without a word of preamble, the elegantly dressed young woman put herself between Brad and Terry and began to gush with praise and excitement. Terry was only too aware of the contrast between herself—still in her walking shorts and hiking boots, grimy and unkempt after their long day—and the elegant young woman. The latter was heavily made up but, Terry had to admit, quite ravishing nonetheless. She said nothing, but only stepped out of the way and listened to the young woman's nonstop monologue.

"Oh, Mr. Andrews, Brad—I feel I know you so well from television that I can call you Brad. . . .

"Certainly, Miss . . ." Brad was reaching into his jacket for a note pad and pen.

"I *told* Joey that it was you, but he said it couldn't be. He said you always wore that trenchcoat and I said no such thing, it *was* you, and if I didn't come right over this second I'd regret it the rest of my life. So I said to Joey, 'You wait right here, I won't be a minute. I'll just go ask for his autograph and tell him what a lovely man I think he is.' Are you going to be in Minneapolis long, Mr. And—*Brad?* If you need someone to show you our lovely town . . ."

"Why, thank you, Miss . . . Miss?"

"Oh. Rose—like the flower. That's Cynthia Rose, *Mrs*. Rose, but don't pay any attention to *that,*" she added with a bold giggle.

Quickly Brad scribbled something on the top slip of paper, then tore it from the pad and pressed it into the elegantly dressed woman's hand. "There you are . . . Cynthia," he said, "and I do thank you for watching."

Fortunately for Terry, who by this time could barely suppress her own laughter, the elevator lurched to a stop just then and both she and Brad swiftly stepped out.

The formally dressed woman hurriedly read the note aloud. "'To my faithful friend Cynthia. In fond remembrance of that night in the elevator. Best wishes always, Brad Andrews.'

"Oh, just wait until the girls see this! Joey's just going to die," she gushed, as the elevator door closed on her happily smiling face.

"You're shameless," Terry said, convulsed with

laughter. She collapsed helplessly into Brad's arms. His strong arms tightened around her waist. She drew back from him quickly, but continued to laugh and shake her head as he took her by the arm and led her down the hallway toward their rooms.

"I have my image to consider," Brad said with great mock dignity, in his best, deepest, TV journalist's voice. "But I think now you see what I mean. How do you think it would be if I took our friend Cynthia up on her offer of the grand tour, and how long would it be before it got into all the papers?"

"And, most importantly, how long would it take for Joey to find you?" Terry added with a laugh.

Brad snorted with pleasure at their shared good humor. "That's just what I'm talking about," he said. "I can practically see the headlines now. . . . Ah, 710 and 712. Here we are. These are our rooms."

Terry took the key that he proffered and slipped it into the lock. With her hand still on the doorknob, she turned back to him. "Do you think you can find your way back down to the restaurant without being waylaid by any more excited fans?" she asked with an impish smile.

Brad was standing scant inches from her again, but this time Terry didn't let herself concentrate on the serious look that had returned to his face. She paid no attention to the intent way he looked down at her, the sudden set of his lips, or the way his nostrils were slightly flared.

"Think you can do that without getting into trouble?" she repeated gaily.

Brad nodded; he seemed on the verge of stepping toward her. "Good," Terry said in the same bright tone of voice. "I'll have a quick bath and meet you down there after I've changed." She turned the door handle and stepped back at the same time. "Bye," she added in a small coquettish voice, leaving Brad to stare at the closing door with his famous journalist's laser-beam eyes.

After the hikes through the Illinois woods and the two tiring flights aboard the small cramped aircraft, the bath in the enormous sunken tub was pure ecstasy!

When she was done, Terry grabbed a towel and patted herself dry in front of the full-length mirror in the steamy, black and white tiled bathroom. She took five extra minutes to put her lissome athlete's body through several basic dance exercises and yoga stretches, a long-standing habit that helped smooth out the tensions and restore her vigor at the end of a long day.

"Still in pretty good shape," she told herself when she had finished, appraising her mirror image and patting her flat, muscular stomach.

Then, because she was in a playful mood and wanted to be as comfortable as possible, she slipped into her black moire silk evening jumper, which she wore over a white silk blouse and with open-toed high heels. The outfit was essentially shapeless, she knew, and it completely hid her long legs and the curves of her supple body. Terry thought this was probably for the best, given the electricity that had seemed to arc between her and Brad at times during the day, but she also knew that the material had a way of catching the light and making it dance that could be more exciting by far than any tight, black crepe evening dress.

In the elevator on her way down to the restaurant to meet Brad, Terry found another surprise. When the door whooshed open, standing alone was a tall, thin, olive-skinned man in a white linen suit and a dark tie. His wavy black hair, aquiline nose and prominent cheekbones all suggested the Latin Lover, an image that was reinforced by his tinted sunglasses and black, patent leather shoes. When she stepped inside, his frank studied gaze moved up her body and over her face like a caress.

A moment later, when he spoke, Terry was not disappointed. "Excusa me, young lady," he said in a thick Italian-accented basso. "I have just arrived today in this fair town from Milano, and I think that perhaps you can perhaps suggest to me a risstorante, no?"

Terry turned and favored the tall Italian with a small smile. "I'm told the hotel has quite a good restaurant," she said politely. "It's called the Normandy Room, I believe, and it's still open. You might want to give it a try."

"Thank you, signorina. You know, when I leave Milano this morning, my friends they—how you say?—'tease' me; they say, 'Fredo, you go to this Mini-a-polis, you find there a—how you say?—'Nordic goddessa' and you fall in love and never come back. I think they make fun of poor Alfredo. I never believe that what they say comes true on this, my first night," he said in a reverent hush.

Terry was amused, but not displeased by this European come-on. "Why, thank you, Alfredo; how nice of you to say so. But I'm not Nordic, and I'm certainly no goddess. In fact, like yourself, I'm only a visitor to this city."

Undeterred, Alfredo considered this piece of information to be just the opportunity he needed.

"Then, signorina, perhaps you will accompany me to dinner, perhaps you too are alone in a strange town."

"No, I'm with a gentleman," replied Terry, thoroughly enjoying herself and the adulation of this handsome stranger. "But thank you for asking, Alfredo. I hope you enjoy your dinner—and find your Nordic goddess," she added as the elevator came to a stop and the door opened. "Goodbye."

"Goodbye, beautiful signorina."

She walked jauntily across the lobby to the Normandy Room, imagining with a certain pleasure the morose, hang-dog look with which the handsome Alfredo watched her leave.

The Normandy Room—dimly lighted, decorated in dark woods and leathers, with shields, banners and heraldic crests lining its walls—lived up to its name. With a theatrical flourish, the maître d' took Terry to a secluded, candlelit back table where Brad—now wearing a dark blue suit and a powder blue, open-necked shirt—was patiently waiting.

The table was covered by fine linen on which were laid gleaming silverware and cut crystal; next to it on a small serving cart waited a magnum of iced champagne in a shiny silver bucket. Smoothly, the maître d' pulled out a high-backed walnut chair for Terry, then silently opened the champagne and poured out two glasses.

"May I begin serving?" he asked.

"In a few minutes," Brad replied, dismissing the man with a wave of his hand.

Since she had arrived, he hadn't once taken his eyes off her, looking at her in a way that sent flutters running up and down her spine. This wasn't the alternately appraising and imploring look that the Italian had just given her. No, this was a look that drank her in, the look of a man etching into his memory a face that he was afraid he might not see again, the look that a prisoner might cast at a seldom-seen glimpse of sky. . . .

"Brad, you're staring at me in the strangest way. . . ."

He shook his head as if breaking free from a spell. "I'm sorry, I—"

"Is that your smoldering, sexy journalist's look?" she teased, hoping to lighten the suddenly portentous atmosphere between them.

"No, not at all. We've been so busy today, running from one place to another, and you've been so insistent on the 'business' at hand, that I just felt like I hadn't *really* looked at you, that this was the first time practically. . . ."

"But we *are* here for business," Terry reminded soberly, even though what she really wanted to do at that moment was to return Brad's look, intensity for intensity, and ask him what did he think, now that he could take a good look, of what he saw.

"I know," Brad conceded, "but it's not what I expected." He lifted his champagne glass. "I guess I have no choice but to propose a toast to the start of a good collaboration, even though what I want to drink to is the most beautiful—"

"Brad!" Terry cautioned.

"—the most beautiful woman in the world!"

"To our book," Terry said firmly, lifting her own glass.

"Okay then, to *The Heartland*—and a new beginning."

Terry clinked her glass with his. "That I can drink

to," she said, taking a small sip. She put down the glass and rubbed the tip of her nose. "The bubbles," she explained. "It happens every time."

Brad smiled fondly. "I remember," he said quietly, the voltage increasing again in the look he gave her.

Terry looked around the room, scrutinizing her surroundings so she wouldn't have to meet Brad's gaze. She took another small sip of the champagne. The restaurant was almost empty, she noticed, except there, on the other side of the room...

Terry leaned forward confidentially. "Brad," she whispered, "that woman and her husband, the one you gave an autograph to in the elevator, are having dinner on the other side of the restaurant. *She's* got her back to us, but her husband—"

"Joey."

"Joey keeps giving us these looks that could kill. If she sees you, she'll come right over. There's no telling what Joey will do then...."

"Don't worry," Brad whispered back conspiratorially. "I fixed it with the maître d'. I slipped him some money so he'll keep an eye out and tell anyone who heads this way that we don't want to be disturbed. He said he'd be discreet."

"Oh." Terry leaned back in her chair, slightly disappointed by the matter-of-fact way Brad talked about arranging for his privacy. "It never occurred to me that this would be standard procedure. Tell me, what's the going rate for bribing a maître d' to run interference for you?"

Brad shrugged. "It depends—on the city, the restaurant. It's something you get used to doing."

"Poor dear," she said, not at all sympathetic. Terry

took another sip of champagne as another couple was led into the restaurant. When she saw that the man was Alfredo, and that he had a somewhat stocky blond woman on his arm, she giggled with pleasurable surprise.

Brad turned around in his seat to follow her gaze. "Who's *that?*" he asked, turning back to face her with a scowl on his handsome face.

"Oh, just someone *I* met in the elevator," she said flirtatiously. "Someone in *my* fan club."

"What?"

She raised her champagne glass. "Just someone looking for a Nordic goddess who settled for a Valkyrie," she said, laughing.

"What?"

"Now, don't get bothered. He's just a foreigner who wanted directions to a good restaurant."

"Well, if you ask me he looks like—"

"Bradford Andrews, don't you dare!"

Brad took a deep breath and gave her a small, chagrined smile. "Now it's getting more like old times, with every man in sight panting after you. . . ."

Terry laughed. "And you, my impetuous knight, ready to fight them all."

Brad laughed along with her. "Shall we eat?" he asked.

Terry looked around. "There aren't any menus."

"We don't need them," he replied, with a nod toward a waiter. "I've already ordered your favorite dinner."

"Already ordered? Really, Brad, I'm not that hungry and it's far too late at night..."

"But you've got to keep up your strength," he protested. "We've got another long day tomorrow, and after what happened this afternoon . . ."

"This afternoon?"

"I thought you were going to faint, back there in the woods. . . ."

"Such concern!"

"I'm serious. You have to be careful."

"But Brad, don't you have girls swooning at your feet all the time?" she teased.

"C'mon, Terry," he said gruffly, "be sensible."

"You of all people should know that I'm nothing if not that," she replied blithely. She was pleased by this show of worry and also aware that the champagne was making her feel giddy. "Well, maybe you're right. Maybe I should have something after all. My 'favorite dinner,' you say. Are you telling me that after all these years you *still* remember what that is?"

"Like it was yesterday," Brad replied earnestly. "I ordered a small romaine and tomato salad, fresh salmon broiled in lemon butter, asparagus spears so lightly steamed that they're still crisp, with just a dab of hollandaise, the excellent native wild rice," he enumerated, as the waiters arrived, as if on cue, with the first of the simple but elegant dishes that sounded so mouth-watering. Brad was right, Terry realized, it *was* her favorite dinner. "And for dessert . . ."

Terry dabbed at her mouth with the napkin. "That was delicious, especially the mousse," she said, as the dessert plates were being cleared away. "I just couldn't finish those last few bites though. It's so light but scandalously rich; I'll have to hike all day just to walk it off."

Brad sighed. "I suppose we should turn in, although I hate to have today end. It's something I've been looking forward to for such a long time. . . .

"Still, Rick will be here to pick us up at eight in the morning for the drive up to the waterway," he added grudgingly, tapping out in a silver ashtray the aromatic Meerschaum he'd been puffing. "Shall we go upstairs?"

Terry nodded compliantly and they both got up to leave. She noticed that the restaurant was empty of other diners, and that the waiters and busboys were already putting out fresh linen and silver for the next day; she was pleased that there were no hysterical fans for Brad or lovesick lotharios for her to contend with.

As the maître d' bowed and thanked them out of the darkened restaurant, with many fervent wishes for their returning patronage, Brad slipped his arm around Terry's waist. For just a fraction of a second she stiffened at his touch. But the gesture seemed so innocent and right, so reminiscent of how they used to walk around together in the old days, that Terry relaxed and let her body lean closer against his.

Wordlessly they strolled slowly across the unoccupied, well-appointed lobby, going deliberately, as if both wanted to prolong the moment, past the overstuffed chairs and couches, past the ferns and potted plants, past the leather banquettes and wooden benches, making their way to the elevators. As they entered the waiting elevator, Terry noticed that the only other person in the quiet hotel lobby—the elderly, white-haired night clerk behind the big mahogany counter—was favoring them with the same broad, beneficent smile with which he must have blessed generations of young lovers. Terry smiled to herself at the thought; a warm glow welled up inside her, a warm glow that couldn't be accounted for by the hot bath, the cold champagne, or even the delicious dinner.

All too soon they were in front of her door. With a start, as if suddenly waking from an achingly wonderful dream, Terry realized that her hand had gone around Brad's back and that her head was leaning against his shoulder; unthinkingly, automatically, she pulled away and quickly opened the door.

"Goodnight, Brad. Let's meet downstairs in the coffee shop, a little before eight in the morning—"

"Wait!" His hand gripped her upper arm tightly, keeping her from disappearing inside the darkened room. There was anger in his voice, just barely under control as he spoke. "I don't know what you think you're pulling," he spat out through clenched teeth, "running hot and cold with me all day and all night like this. If you're trying to get back at me for what happened years ago, then say so. Yell at me, do anything!"

"Brad, I never—"

"Don't tell me you don't feel anything, don't tell me you don't remember anything, don't tell me that it's all business. . . ."

His pressure on her arm increased. "Brad, don't," Terry protested, "you're hurting me." But his grip only tightened; slowly he began to pull her toward him.

"These aren't kids' games we're playing now." His handsome face, world famous as the symbol of calm and control, was contorted by rage and emotions that neither of them dared name. He wrapped her in his arms and crushed her against his chest. As he lowered his head toward hers, his breath was coming in explosive little puffs. "And even kids get a goodnight kiss. . . ."

At first, his lips just brushed against hers; then with a rising fury, his mouth pressed down. Resistance was more than useless.

This time the warm glow flowered into flame. With a small moan, Terry let her mouth open and pushed up against him, meeting his passion with her own. She pressed her body against his, letting herself glory for just a moment in the feeling of his muscular legs, his insistent loins pushing against her own. He kissed her face, her ears, her neck. She moaned with pleasure as his encircling hands raced past the small of her back. Then he raised his head, whispered her name and kissed her hard on the lips. She responded greedily to his probing tongue. They kissed, and they kissed, and the world seemed to go round and round. . . .

Until at last she heard the small warning voice in her mind—*The promise, Terry, the promise!*—and she pulled herself free from this vortex of delight.

"No!" She shook her head from side to side so violently that her flaxen tresses whipped across her eyes. Then she pushed Brad away, both hands straining against his chest. "We're not kids anymore, and we have to stop now. No, no more!"

"Terry—"

"No, Brad, no more! Leave me alone." She stepped away from him, back into her open doorway.

"I'm sorry, Terry, the evening, the champagne. It's just that I thought . . ."

Again she shook her head and held up her hand,

warning him to stop. "No, don't say it. It's my fault too. Let's just forget it happened; let's just write it off to old times."

"Terry, please—"

"No. We'll start off fresh in the morning—a clean slate—just like this never happened," she said in a rush.

As she closed the door, Brad said in a low, hoarse voice, "I'll be nearby if you need me. . . ."

Terry leaned against the inside of the closed door for several long moments. She was trembling and felt feverish. Then quickly, without turning on the lights, she peeled off her clothes and crawled into bed, hoping for the blissful release of sleep.

But thinking of him there, so close, in the very next room, she tossed and turned all night. Sleep seemed impossible, and didn't come finally until the coral light of the Spring dawn peeked through the cracks of her shuttered window.

chapter 4

Poor Rick! Terry said to herself sympathetically.

Dressed in his chinos and a football jersey, his chauffeur's cap perched jauntily on his head, he had come bouncing into the coffee shop, stopping momentarily to sniff the aromatic morning smells of just-brewed coffee and freshly baked Danish pastry, before walking over to her little table and giving her a big, cheerful *"Hello!"* She could tell he was excited by the prospect of another day with his hero.

"Hello," she had snapped back at him in a curt, drop-dead tone, and he had immediately retreated two paces, backing away from her as if struck.

Now she lowered her sunglasses and gave him a rueful little smile. "Sorry, a sleepless night," she apologized. "It's not your fault. Please, sit down."

Gingerly he took the chair across from her. "I kin understand that," he allowed, in the open, uninflected voice of a native Midwesterner.

Again Terry had dressed for the outdoor workday, wearing a pair of scruffy Adidas without socks, faded blue jeans, and a light blue halter camisole. Just to add a little class, she had told herself while putting it on, and to get a bit of a tan. Draped over the arm of her chair was a navy blue cotton windbreaker, its many pockets filled with rolls of film, tanning lotion, and her trusty light meter.

From the open-mouthed way young Rick was staring at her bare shoulders, Terry could tell just how little it would take to make the young man forget all about his idol Brad; it was lucky for them both, she thought, that she was neither a cradle robber nor a gold digger.

Still staring at her shoulders, Rick reached into his pants pocket and pulled out a small packet of pink and blue slips. "For Mr. Andrews, ma'am," he said, placing them in front of her. "Messages forwarded to him from his New York office."

Terry pushed the packet back toward the center of the table, irritated at the thought that the young chauffeur assumed she was some sort of traveling secretary or, what was worse, thought she was Brad's traveling "companion."

"Give them to the Great Man yourself." She took a gulp from the glass of orange juice in front of her, noticing as she did that the top message in the thick stack advised Brad that someone named Frieda had called. Undoubtedly another fan club member, she thought ruefully.

Rick gave the messages a perplexed stare. "Huh? I don't understand," he mumbled. "They said at the office to make sure he got 'em."

Terry slipped her dark, oval sunglasses back on. "I'm a photographer," she said in a severe, distant voice, "a professional photographer. Right now I've got an exhibit at an important gallery in Chicago.

"Mr. Andrews—*Brad*—and I are doing a book together. I am *not* his secretary, nor do I pass messages on to him. I hope I make myself clear. There is no reason in the world for you to *presume* anything else," she added, realizing that it might sound to more sophisticated ears than this boy's that she was protesting too much. "That's all. Period."

Rick looked stricken. "Gee, I'm sorry. I really didn't mean—"

Terry waved his apology aside. "I know you didn't do it intentionally; it's just that it's the kind of casual assumption that I—or any woman, or any *person,* for that matter—finds insulting."

Rick hung his head. "Yes, ma'am."

Terry sighed. *Poor Rick,* she said to herself for the second time in the last five minutes, *just trying to do his job, impress his hero, and he runs right up against my offended honor*. "Don't worry about it," she said consolingly. "It was an easy mistake to make, really, and I shouldn't have been so hard on you for it. I guess I really am in a foul mood after not sleeping well last night.

"So, really, don't worry about it. I won't say a

word to Brad and we'll just forget that it ever happened. Okay?"

"Gee, thanks, ma'am." Rick said, a look of pure relief on his face.

"Terry," she said with a smile.

"Gee, thanks, Terry," Rick repeated, just as Brad came through the coffee shop door and walked over to their table.

He was wearing a long sleeve madras shirt, tan pleated pants and brown Topsiders without socks, but he didn't look nearly as chipper as his outfit. His eyes were bleary and, as soon as he sat down, he took out his aviator sunglasses from his shirt pocket and put them on.

"A sleepless night," he grunted to the thoroughly perplexed Rick, who seemed too intimidated by his journalist-hero's presence to do more than just push the packet of messages toward him.

"For you, sir, from New York," he said deferentially.

Brad glanced at the top two messages, then put the rest into his shirt pocket without looking at them. "'Frieda called' and 'Your mother called.'" Brad shook his head in bemused amazement. "How do you like that? They track me halfway across the country just to tell me that I got calls from my mother and from my barber."

Terry was pleased at the information that Frieda was Brad's barber and not another one of the many women who apparently were forever throwing themselves at his feet, but she said nothing. Instead, she finished the last of her orange juice, put down her glass, and asked, "Are you going to have any breakfast, Brad?"

"No, I'm not hungry," he replied brusquely, adding in a sour tone, whose significance Rick could not hope to guess, "Besides, we do have lots of 'business' to attend to today."

The ride north was uneventful, but nonetheless filled with residues of tension from the night before. Terry shared the Cadillac's big back seat with Brad, but they might as well have been in separate cars. He stared out one window or busied himself by reading his notes for the day's narrative while she stared out the other window.

From time to time, Terry replayed the delirious events of the previous evening in her mind and wondered what else she could have done. *Nothing,* she concluded to herself. *She was friendly but she didn't lead him on, and she did try to keep attentive to her promise and his engagement. If only he had cooperated, instead of turning on the charm. . . .* She shook her head, resolving to herself that from now on she would ignore those feelings—strong emotions and even stronger physical desires—that he still could evoke in her so easily.

Straight up Interstate 35 to Pine City they went, then Rick turned the big black limousine east and drove on to where the Minnesota-Wisconsin border met the St. Croix National Scenic Riverway. From here, the wild river meandered southwest for more than a hundred miles, forming the borderline between the two states.

"Here's the plan, Rick," Brad explained as they neared their destination, while Terry stared somewhat pensively at the scenery flashing by outside the limousine's tinted side window. "You drop us off at the boat dock. We're going to canoe down river, stopping here and there to take pictures and make notes." Brad pulled out a map and a red pen from a small cabinet in the Cadillac's side door. "You drive south until you get here," he said, circling a point a few miles north of the St. Croix Falls. "There's another boat dock and a little roadside inn where you can wait for us. Then all you have to do is drive us back into town, to our hotel, and pick us up once again tomorrow morning for the ride out to the airport."

"Is that all, sir?" Rick sounded disappointed.

"I'm afraid so."

"Is there anything I can do for you while I'm waiting? Help you with research or anything like that?"

"Thank you, but no. We shouldn't be back before midafternoon at the very earliest, so it's a free afternoon for you."

"Oh—and in the morning, sir, is there anything I can do for you tomorrow?"

"Not a thing, Rick," Brad said breezily. "We're going on to northern Michigan in the morning. I'm afraid that's a little out of your territory, even given your station manager's generosity with your time."

"Yes, sir," Rick agreed glumly. "I don't think Mr. Moorhouse would like that."

Despite her clouded mood, Terry smiled at this little exchange. The young chauffeur's eagerness to please, his obvious drive to get ahead and better himself, reminded her of the young man that Brad had once been. He, too, had been eager for success, but he had always possessed qualities that young Rick, and almost everyone else, seemed to lack. For one thing, there was his physical "presence," a charismatic aura like a spotlight that had marked him from the earliest times as a darling of fate, someone whose destiny was to hold the rapt attention of others; it was *this* quality, and *not* the love that they had once shared, Terry told herself, that still made Brad so irresistible. For another thing, there was his fabulous luck, the quality of being in the right place at the right time that in a few short years had brought him from the ivy-covered gateways of the college campus to the hushed corridors of journalistic power in gleaming New York skyscrapers.

Without such good fortune could Rick—or anyone—get so far so fast? Terry wondered. While she was musing to herself about the mysterious workings of fate and destiny, the car pulled up at the dilapidated wooden boat dock beside the slow-moving river. Soon she and Brad, sitting at opposite ends of a long aluminum canoe with their equipment between them, had pushed off from the shore and were waving to Rick, who was waving forlornly back at them from the riverbank. Within minutes, the current had carried them around a bend and they left all signs of civilization behind. Once again, they were the only two people in sight.

The sun broke through the morning mist. Terry pulled off her windbreaker, exposing her bare shoulders to the warming rays. She squinted up at the light. It was going to be a beautiful day after all.

They had been drifting downstream for well over an hour, letting the current carry them, exchanging occasional brief comments and pleasantries in the hushed tones appropriate to this quiet, peaceful, scenic waterway.

Brad was in the rear of the canoe, the paddle across

his lap, his cassette recorder beside him on the wooden bench. From time to time, he would put the paddle into the blue, silver-flecked stream and correct their drifting course with one or two expert strokes.

Terry was seated on the front bench, with her back to the canoe's prow. On her lap was the Leica, ready to capture those fleeting moments that would illustrate the river's beauty to the world.

Already she had snapped shots of a gossamer-winged dragonfly skimming like a shooting star just above the sparkling water, of a solemn-looking great blue heron observing them from its one-legged perch on a tree limb jutting out from the water near the shore, and of a line of tall, steep rocks lining a section of the riverbank.

As she had framed the shot of the rocks, Brad had turned on his recorder and commented, "This section of the St. Croix is lined by massive stone slabs called *dalles*. These great, weathered-looking slate gray rocks reminded the early fur traders who once plied this river of the paving stones used to construct the magnificent cathedrals in their native France, so they named the rocks *dalles* after the French word meaning 'flagstones.'"

Down the river they drifted, past woods aflame with the bright colors of Spring, where it was all that Terry could do to try to keep up with the profusion of idyllic scenes: a copper-tinted stand of oaks, gold-leafed birches and rust-red maples, a field of pink and white trillium, a carpet of riotously colored wildflowers just glimpsed behind a veil of waving marsh grass—all these quickly came and went.

Brad continued to whisper into his cassette recorder: "As a boy, I would come with my parents to this river, where the Sioux, the Ojibwa and the Chippewa once hunted and fished, to enjoy its beauty and peace and serenity. Although my travels as a man have taken me far from this place, I have often thought about the times spent here, both as a boy and as a young man bringing his first love to a treasured private place. . . ."

Terry looked up from her camera long enough to say, "I hope you're going to erase that last little comment."

"Why should I, it's the truth."

"I don't think it's a truth that Sarah McMasters is going to appreciate," Terry replied, quickly twisting in her seat to get a picture of a plump, toothy beaver as it slapped into the water from the nearby bank.

Brad switched off the recorder. "Who cares what she thinks," he said belligerently; "it's *our* book. She can take it or leave it."

They were gliding by a small island in midstream. Terry was about to retort to the effect that Sarah wasn't the only McMasters that Brad should consider, when she saw a potentially great photograph just waiting to be taken among the few birches, pines and oaks that were the island's only vegetation.

"Brad, pull in, quickly. Over there." She pointed to a little inlet, just big enough to nose in their canoe. "There's a shot I want to get on that island."

Quickly, Brad dipped his paddle into the water. With several short, powerful strokes, he turned the canoe against the flow of the current and aimed it expertly into the small opening that Terry had indicated. When the canoe bumped up against the bank, she hopped out and held the bow line until he had jumped out and pulled the canoe up on shore. Then she grabbed her Leica and scrambled up the bank, with Brad following curiously behind her.

The narrow little island was only a couple of hundred feet in length, and no more than thirty feet in width. At its center, rising far above the other trees that nestled all around it, was a tall, solitary Norway spruce, its reddish-brown trunk climbing nearly one hundred feet into the clear Spring sky.

At the top of the bank, Terry paused to take several shots of the entire panorama: the trees of various shapes, sizes and colors, all harmoniously clustered together, the peaceful blue-green river flowing past the island, the lush far shore. Then she and Brad tiptoed through the tall grasses and dead branches that covered this part of the island, slowly making their way toward the lone spruce.

"Look," Terry whispered, as she positioned herself for the shot. She pointed up at the tree trunk, about fifteen feet over their heads, at a small round hole that was the entrance to a hollow in the bole of the spruce tree. The open space was the size of a large hand mirror; filling it, looking unblinkingly down at them, was a round, pixie-like face, with huge yellow eyes peeking out from behind what appeared to be a feathery, silver mask over a blue gray bald head.

"WHOOO?" the pixie face seemed to ask, as if challenging their right to trespass on its domain.

Quickly, Terry snapped the first of several photographs.

Brad whispered into her ear. "That's a saw-whet owl. The Indians used to say they brought good luck."

While Terry continued to shoot, the owl, with great dignity, used its beak to pull itself up out of the hollow. It hopped from the lip of the hole to a nearby branch. There it stood for a moment, regarding them with its great gleaming eyes, while it smoothed its ruffled feathers and slowly stretched out its gray-tipped, reddish-brown wings that were exactly the same color as the tree trunk.

"WHOOO?" it asked again. With a flap of its wings, it hopped out into space. Its wings beat the air twice before the owl caught an air current and glided away. Soon it was lost from sight.

Terry was delighted. "I got all of that," she announced happily, "the little round face peeking out of the hole, the bird preening itself then flying away—everything!"

"That's great," Brad agreed enthusiastically. "You know, if that little bird looks as cute on film as it did just now, I think one of those photos would make a terrific cover picture for the book."

Terry was relaxing with Brad for almost the first time that day. "Say, that's not a bad idea at all, Mr. Andrews," she said with mock formality. "You keep that up and we'll make a darn good art editor out of you yet."

Brad chuckled warmly. He slipped a friendly arm around Terry's shoulder and said, "What do you say we have lunch here? I had Rick pack us a little ice chest. It's in the canoe."

Terry was about to shrug off the friendly embrace, but she decided not to spoil the moment. "Okay," she said simply, warming to the touch of Brad's strong hand on the bare skin of her upper arm.

When they returned to the little inlet where their canoe was tied, Brad pulled out a large plaid blanket and spread it on a patch of bare ground. Then he brought over the ice chest, opened it, and began to take out its contents.

First he opened a bottle of inexpensive California red wine and filled a plastic cup. "M'lady," he said, offering the wine to Terry, who quickly demurred.

"No thanks, Brad, it's too early in the day for me," she said, remembering only too well what the champagne at the hotel restaurant the night before had done to her good judgment and will power. "Got anything else to drink?"

Brad was obviously disappointed that she wasn't drinking, but he said nothing. "Oh, a little apple juice, some French mineral water," he said in a tone that was only slightly forced. "I'll drink the wine," he added. "Mustn't let the grape go to waste."

Terry helped herself to a small bottle of Perrier and rummaged around in the ice chest, examining the waxpaper-wrapped sandwiches and the selection of fresh fruit that was packed there. Finally, she settled on an apple and two small cucumber sandwiches to go with her mineral water.

The sun felt warm, its dappled rays reaching through the vaulted tree branches to caress her skin, so she took off her shoes and rolled the legs of her jeans up to her knees.

After a moment, Brad unbuttoned his shirt. Terry tried not to pay attention to the broad, muscular chest he bared to the afternoon sun. Instead, she watched the courtship play of two nearly transparent insects as they danced just over the water and the colorful, scarlet and gold flashes as birds chased each other through the air. A pair of majestic swans bobbed by the island and floated lazily downstream.

Terry continued to munch on her sandwiches, watching the peaceful, ever-changing scene and listening to the soothing sounds—rustling leaves, lapping water—of the natural world all around her. Beside her, Brad poured himself a second cup of wine and stretched out on his side. As he continued to drink, Terry found herself more and more aware of his nearness and the intensity of his concentration. He was not, she realized, gazing upon the same natural wonders that she was enjoying. Self-consciously, she shifted her place on the blanket, moving a few inches further away from him.

She asked him a question to break the increasing tension she felt. "About the owl," she began. "You said something about the Indians thinking it was good luck. Is there a story there?"

Brad downed the last of the contents of his cup and poured himself another. "It's one of the old legends that my father always used to tell us," he said. "We'd come up here, go canoeing and fishing, and he'd tell story after story about the Indians and the settlers who used to live in this place.

"Well, one of his favorites was about that little saw-whet owl we just saw. It seems that so many owls live along the river that the Indians built up a whole bunch of lore about them—different stories and different beliefs to go with the different species."

Brad sat up. "It's kind of interesting, actually; I'll have to remember to put this in the book. Did that little owl remind you of anybody?" he asked. "You know, the baby face, the chubby body, the wings?"

Terry shook her head. "No, nobody that I can think of."

"My father pointed out this resemblance," Brad continued, "and it's pretty obvious once you know about it—and quite a coincidence, too."

"What is?" Terry asked, growing impatient with the roundabout story.

"That the owl looks just like a little cupid, only the Sioux couldn't have known anything about that particular legend."

Terry thought about this for a moment. "You know you're right," she remarked with some amazement. "It *did* look like a little cherubic cupid. How do you like that."

Brad took another sip of wine. "I told you it was obvious as soon as you knew," he said a little thickly, nodding his head for emphasis as he spoke.

"And what's the Indian legend? Is it like the cupid story?" Terry asked curiously.

"Very much so," Brad replied. "The Indians believed that when two young lovers stole away for a rendezvous, it was great luck to meet one of these little birds in the forest. In fact, they believed that the lovers' future good fortune was assured if they—let me put this as delicately as possible—'made love' underneath the perch of one of these owls.

"They believed that the gods of the hunt and the harvest would always smile on such a couple," he added in a whisper, leaning toward Terry. "They also believed that if the lovers kissed and embraced after seeing one of these cupid-birds their futures were assured."

Terry stood up before Brad could go any further. "I think it's time to be on our way again," she said quickly.

Brad, too, stood up. To Terry, he definitely seemed tipsy. "What about the little bird?" he asked. "Are we going to let all that good luck go to waste?"

Terry picked up her Leica. She put the camera protectively around her neck. "I'm not superstitious," she said firmly. "And I'm sure you'll be up here again with someone else who'll fall for that line," she added. Brad could bring Caroline McMasters. Then that bit of Indian lore would be much more appropriate.

Something smoldered in the look Brad was giving her—something that spoke of longing and desire and long-thwarted passion. They were several miles farther downstream; and as the shadows lengthened and the sun fell, its dark red orb seeming to touch his broad shoulders, the silence between them deepened, while the tension grew to a fever pitch.

At first, Brad's look had warmed her. If it hadn't been for her promise, if he hadn't been engaged, if she hadn't been all too aware of her need to avoid joining that army of women who were in willing thrall to this Media Hero, she might have responded to all that this steady, unwavering look promised. But she didn't. And as the moments passed, Terry—for the first time since the beginning of her trip with him—was afraid.

At last, Brad seemed unable to stand it any longer. His voice, breaking the long silence between them, was strained and sounded desperate. "What torture it is to be so close to you," he declared passionately, "alone with you, in these same places where once we knew such bliss. I didn't think it would be this bad, but it's worse than I could ever imagine.

"Terry," he blurted out, "I *must* have you! I *know* you feel the same way too!" Without warning, he suddenly lunged across the canoe toward her.

"Brad, no!" she cried out, putting out her hands to keep him away. But it was too late. One long, crouching step had carried him to her.

Terry tried to fight him, flailing her arms and kicking her legs out at him, but his power swept her protests aside. He pushed against her, his body finding hers; cruel lips took possession of her own. One hand pinned her arms, while the other roughly explored her arched body. Still she fought.

The canoe rocked ever more violently from side to side; water splashed in.

"No, Brad, no!" Terry screamed, but to no avail. Then it happened.

The canoe pitched sharply to one side, almost going over. Brad's surprised effort to regain the balance overcompensated for the sharp rocking motion. As if in slow motion, the canoe dipped back again and rolled over, throwing them both into the icy water.

After the first shock, Terry came slowly back to the surface. She was a good swimmer and she wasn't angry, really; she was even a little amused by the Keystone Kops aspect of the overturned canoe, until she remembered her cameras. Everything—except one exposed roll of film in the little watertight container tucked safely into the pocket of her jeans—had gone over the side with them!

She saw Brad in the water several feet away. "My

stuff!" she yelled to him, swallowing a mouthful of water. "All the cameras are gone!"

She didn't really see the long, black, spiky object bearing down on her like some great prehistoric reptile. She only saw the look of terror on Brad's face and heard his warning cry, then it was there. . . .

The jagged end of the forty-foot-long trunk of an oak tree, blackened by lightning, just missed her head as it was propelled downstream by the current. She ducked underwater and tried to swim out of harm's way, but it was too late.

A branch caught the strap of the Leica still around her neck and pulled her back.

The camera's strap was a noose. The more she struggled, the tighter became the tree's deadly embrace.

For just an instant she fought free to the surface—long enough to take a single ragged breath and to glimpse Brad's powerful form swimming rapidly through churning water toward her, something silver gleaming in his outstretched hand. Then the great tree gave a lazy quarter turn in the water and pulled her effortlessly far below the surface once again.

The green water all around her turned to a blackness before her eyes.

Then Brad was there, diving to her, air bubbles streaming from his mouth and nose. One strong hand grasped the tangled strap, the other cut through it with a shining knife. And suddenly she was free!

They broke through the surface together. With one hand under her chin, Brad towed Terry's limp form to the shore and dragged her up on the sandy bank.

Hovering over her outstretched body, he kept repeating, "Are you okay? Are you okay?"

Coughing and gasping, with one arm around Brad's neck for support, she stood up. "Yes," she whispered, tears streaming down her face. "Yes." Then her knees gave way, and she sagged into Brad's strong, cradling arms.

"Oh my lord, Maybelle, will you look at who that is!" The two matronly, white-haired tourists, in summery flower print dresses, stopped taking pictures of each other and stared over at the battered pickup truck that had just pulled up next to the big, black Cadillac parked at the side of the road. "It's him, Maybelle, I swear it's him!"

Wet, bedraggled, shivering after the ride in the open back of the truck, Brad and Terry climbed out and thanked the grizzled old farmer who had stopped to give them a ride.

Clutching two blankets, Rick ran to them. He was nearly hysterical from worry. "The canoe . . . We fished it out of the water," he babbled. "We were going to call the police—we feared the worst!" Rick threw a blanket over Brad's shoulders, then the other over Terry's. "Are you all right, sir?" he asked.

"Yes, yes, no need to worry. Just a boating accident. One of those things," Brad mumbled.

After conferring together, one of the two white-haired elderly ladies marched boldly over to Brad and tugged on the end of the blanket.

"Excuse me, young man," she said in a reedy voice, "but are you who Maybelle and I think you are?"

"Yes, ma'am, I'm afraid I am."

"Landsake. What are *you* doing *here?*"

"Just on vacation, ma'am," Brad replied courteously, pulling the blanket tighter around his shoulders.

The other tourist lady had been listening shyly to this exchange; now she, too, got up enough courage to join in. "Why, whatever happened to you?" she asked.

"Just a little boating accident, ma'am," Brad explained. "Nothing to worry about." Over his shoulder, he added to Rick, "Let's get going before both Terry and I catch pneumonia."

This was a sentiment Terry agreed with completely. As she flopped into the back seat of the car, she was more than a little irritated to see Brad stop to autograph the piece of paper that the second lady thrust up at him. "To Maybelle and Lily," he said as he wrote, "who saw me at my worst and who I hope will continue to tune in to watch me at my best. With regards, Bradford Andrews."

"So kind to his admirers," Terry observed caustically when Brad finally got into the limousine. She shook her wet hair vigorously enough so that several drops hit Brad full in the face.

The limousine roared off, with Rick driving as if he would set a world record getting them back to their hotel. "Are all your belongings gone?" he asked solicitously as they sped down the highway.

Brad replied glumly, "I lost the Swiss pocket knife my father gave me when I was ten."

Terry was outraged. *"What!"*

Soberly and with great sincerity, Brad told her, "I'm terribly sorry that this happened. That kind of stupid accident hasn't happened to me since I was a kid."

"Perhaps it wouldn't have happened if you weren't acting like a kid," Terry shot back. "Your precious Swiss pocket knife, indeed! *All* my cameras are gone!" she added icily.

"Do you know how much they cost?" she continued. "Do you realize how long it took me to save up to buy that equipment?" Terry took a deep breath, determined to stop before she grew shrill or out of control. "Oh, never mind."

She turned her head to the window. They rode the rest of the way back to the hotel in a chilly silence.

The knock at her hotel room door was completely unexpected.

Terry had jumped out of the Cadillac as soon as it stopped at the hotel's front door. She'd slammed the door behind her, leaving Brad and young Rick still in the car, and had gone directly up to her room. She'd put out the "do-not-disturb" sign, locked her door, taken off all her wet clothes and stepped straight into a steaming shower that seemed to wash away all her chills and irritations along with the day's dirt and grime. Afterward, she slipped into her favorite white cotton nightshirt, called room service, and had a bowl of hot tomato soup and a cup of hot buttered rum sent up. Then she flicked on the television; but there was Brad's handsome, earnest face again! Just her luck to turn directly to a rerun of his popular TV show.

Muttering under her breath, she threw back the covers, got back up, and switched off the set. Then came the knock on the door.

"Who is it?" she asked.

"It's me, ma'am, uh, Terry. It's Rick."

"Go away. I'm asleep."

"I've got a package here for you. What do you want me to do with it?"

"Oh, just a second. I'll let you in."

It was several packages that Rick had, as Terry soon found out. He handed her box after box of camera equipment—another Leica, a brand new box camera, a state-of-the-art Minolta XG-M with a 3/5 fps motor drive, a strobe light, a tripod, a light meter—much more, in fact, than she had lost to the river.

"This must have cost thousands!" she gasped.

"Yes, ma'am, Mr. Andrews gave me his very own credit card and instructions not to come back until I had it all. He said money was no object, that I was to get you the best." Rick handed her the last box—long and thin—and a sealed envelope. "He said I was to give you this last, and not to wait for an answer. He said to say he hoped you'd be ready to go again early tomorrow morning on the flight to your next location, but if you weren't he said to say he'd understand. G'night, ma'am." Rick tipped his chauffeur's cap and backed out the door. "I'll see you once again in the morning on the ride to the airport, I hope." And he was gone.

Terry opened the long box. Inside were a dozen blood red, long-stemmed roses. Then she unsealed the envelope. On the card inside Brad had written, "You're absolutely right. I *am* a kid—long on memory and desire, short on patience and smarts. Please forgive me. It will not happen again. Brad."

Terry took out a single red rose. She barely had

enough energy left to put the rest of the roses in a vase on the night table. Still clutching the single rose, she crawled back into bed.

She lay there, musing on the events of the last few days, on Brad's note and her own confused feelings, until she began drifting off to sleep. As her eyes slowly closed, her last waking thought was that she hadn't remembered to lock the door again after Rick's departure.

A gust of wind blew through the diaphanous curtains of her open window, then a creaking at the door. . . . Framed in the doorway, something large, black and scaly loomed in the darkness, and at last she screamed, crying out again and again to Brad to save her. . . .

Terry jolted into wakefulness and Brad *was* there, wrapped in a dark blue bathrobe, leaning over her, holding her gently by the shoulders, whispering to her in the dark.

"It's okay, it's okay," he said over and over again. "It was just a bad dream. You're all right now. I'm here, there's nothing to be afraid of, you can rest. It's okay, it's okay."

"Brad," she said weakly, "it was a horrible nightmare. I was so scared and I couldn't scream."

Gently, he brushed strands of hair from her damp forehead. "I heard you screaming in your sleep," he said. "I thought you called my name. The door was unlocked, so I ran in. . . Terry, I'll sit in that chair on the other side of the room—the yellow wing chair—until you fall asleep. No funny business, I promise. Okay?"

"Okay," Terry agreed in a small voice as Brad

pulled the covers up under her chin. He leaned over and brushed her cheek with his lips.

"Goodnight," he said, walking over and settling into the high-backed chair.

"Goodnight, Brad." Before she again drifted off, Terry whispered, "Brad?"

"Yes," came his deep voice out of the darkness.

"Thanks for all the camera stuff," she said, feeling warm and secure under the covers, with Brad nearby.

"It was nothing, the least I could do after today," he replied from across the room.

"Brad?"

"Yes."

"About tomorrow morning."

"Yes?"

"I'm ready to go on to Michigan, if you still are."

"That's terrific," he said with some emotion. "Now you better get some sleep."

Terry closed her tired eyes and instantly fell into a deep, dreamless sleep. When she awoke, just after dawn, Brad was still sleeping in the wing chair on the other side of her room.

chapter 5

From the very beginning, Terry had been uncertain that she could go through with this part of the trip, and the events of the last few tempestuous days had only increased her doubts. Even at the Minneapolis airport, bidding goodbye to the clearly disappointed Rick, she had hesitated before boarding the Beechcraft. But here she was again, alone in the sky with Brad, flying high over the Great North Woods.

Still, for the first time in their long journey, the atmosphere between them seemed warm and relaxed, as if the long night during which Brad had sat protectively in her hotel room had broken an unspoken constraint, as if it was finally all right to be friends. So, during the long flight to the northeast, when Brad complained of a stiff neck and tired shoulders, Terry had instantly recalled how he had looked curled on the wing chair in her room. Wordlessly, she had slipped into the small space behind the pilot's seat. She had massaged his neck and shoulder muscles until she felt the knots disappear beneath her probing fingers.

"Okay?" she had asked after several minutes, her hands still resting lightly on his shoulders.

"Great," he'd replied, turning his head to the side to kiss her fingertips. "Just lovely."

Then, suddenly trembling, Terry had returned to her place—hastily—to busy herself testing out the new equipment, using her new, powerful wide-angle and telephoto lenses to shoot through the aircraft's window whenever Brad dipped low over the many scenic sights below—anything to keep her mind from thinking about his powerful shoulders and to quiet her racing pulse.

"The Iron Range," he said, and she had snapped away at the barren, terraced ridges below.

They turned east just south of Duluth, skimming over that outstretched finger of Lake Superior pointing to the headwaters of the St. Croix River. "The second largest lake in the world," Brad noted, as Terry took a picture of an ore freighter, looking like a toy ship, far below.

After the Huron Mountains, they followed the winding coastline east. "You know the only larger lake in the world?" Brad asked, a note of wonder in his voice as they passed over the Pictured Rocks area, while Terry took a striking, wide-angle photo of the ancient, gold-tinged bluffs.

"No, what's the only larger lake in the world?"

"The Caspian Sea, that's what. It's a lake by definition, because its surrounded on all sides by land; but it's so big they call it a sea. And Superior isn't much smaller. . . . Imagine that."

On they had gone, flying along the margin between water and land. "Hemingway country," Brad said, pointing down to the meandering river below. "Not the Hemingway of Spain and Africa and such—that all came later. That's the famous Big Two Hearted River down there, the setting for some of his best work."

Terry had snapped away, and not long after Brad had announced, "Seney. Now we're almost there." Once again Terry shot frame after frame of the lonely bogs, the calm lakes and the thick pine forests that comprised the Seney Wildlife Refuge.

"I'm going on to Paradise," Brad remarked with a little grin. "Then I'll turn us around and set down at a little field near the lodge, between Seney and the lake." Which was just what he did, flying low over the bucolic, appropriately named little upper-peninsula town of Paradise, then wheeling around to land within sight of the crashing waves of Lake Superior's southern shore.

They disembarked and, within the hour, a taxi deposited them *there*, at *that* place whose very name brought the dreaded whirl of conflicting feelings to Terry's head and the beating of wild desire to her heart—the Paradise Lodge!

Only a week ago she had been sure that this was one place she would never see again, but fate had brought her back.

The lodge—in Europe, it would have been called a chalet—was just the way she remembered it, its rough-hewn stone walls overgrown with ivy, the sloping wooden beams of the roof hanging over the long front porch. Even stout Mrs. Klaus, the owner's wife, was just the way Terry remembered her, standing at the front door in the same gingham apron, greeting them like long-lost family come back home.

"I don't believe it, she actually remembers us," Terry whispered to Brad, when Frau Klaus's fussing and greeting were over with and they were on their way to change in their adjoining rooms upstairs.

From his doorway, Brad gave her a smile full of good-natured lust. "My dear Theresa," he said, affecting a world-weary, sophisticated tone, "just how many college kids do you suppose they get here who check in without luggage, during a raging blizzard, and then don't leave their room *once* for an entire week? I expect we're a legend around here," he added with a grin.

Terry blushed, smiling back at him in spite of herself. "You know, you could be right," she said, laughing. "This time, though, should do wonders for our reputations. I'll meet you downstairs in twenty minutes."

Inside her cozy little room—the big brass bed, the quilts, the comforters, the rocking chair and the fireplace, were all just as she remembered—Terry continued to smile at the memories even though she still had to deal with the problem of *what to wear*. On the ride over in the battered airport taxi Brad had absolutely *insisted* that the best way to explore the lake shore and the surrounding wilderness was on horseback, at least on this first day of their three-day stay.

He had reminded her of the Klaus's fine stables behind the lodge house and eventually, despite not having the right clothes with her, she had given in.

"I'll just make do," she had said bravely, "besides, you *know* I love to ride. I still go out to the riding club in Evanston every chance I get."

But now, spreading out all her clothes on the bed in her room, Terry was faced with the dismal reality of her depleted wardrobe. Quickly, she made an inventory.

Jeans: still soaked from yesterday.

Walking shorts: missing, probably in her old camera bag at the bottom of the St. Croix.

Culottes: hanging in her closet back home in Chicago.

Blue satin running pants: ditto.

Riding boots or appropriate shoes of any sort: back home too.

What did she have left? Evening clothes, cocktail dresses, sweaters, the sundress she was wearing...

Terry sighed. She looked at herself in the long mirror on the back of the bathroom door, at the sundress—navy blue with a white rose print—and the flimsy leather sandals she'd put on in the morning.

This *does* have possibilities, she thought to herself, putting a couple of rolls of film into the deep front pockets of the dress. She kicked off the sandals and picked them up in one hand.

Might as well shock Mrs. Klaus all over again, she thought mischievously, *after all it's the only practical thing left to do.* Gaily she grabbed her new camera bag and waltzed out the door, padding barefoot down the stairs.

A few minutes later, after stopping in at the stables,

she met Brad on the front porch.

One look at him standing there, resplendent in his riding clothes, with leather saddle bags over one arm, told Terry that this must have been what he had in mind from the very first. Otherwise, how did he come to have with him the tan oxford cloth polo shirt, the rust-colored jodhpurs and the dark brown, knee-length riding boots? For some reason the sight of him in those dashing clothes added to the bold and giddy frame of mind in which Terry found herself.

"My, don't *you* look flashy," she said admiringly.

"Thank you, m'dear," Brad replied, affecting a clipped British accent. He looked askance at her bare feet and her insubstantial dress. "You're lookin' kinda flashy yourself, kid," he joked, switching to Brooklynese, "although not *exactly* ready for riding to the hounds."

Just then the stableboy brought their mounts around. For Brad there was a high-stepping black stallion with a long, silky black mane. The horse's thoroughbred lines and aristocratic manner indicated that it was at least part Arabian. The saddle-soaped English riding saddle on its back seemed entirely appropriate to Brad's chic riding outfit.

Terry's animal was a broad-chested bay, with a dark mane and tail and white markings on its feet. As she had requested, the stableboy had placed on her horse an old and worn Western saddle with a soft leather seat and had tied red silk scarves around the stirrups to protect her bare feet.

While Brad tied on the saddle bags, Terry stuffed her sandals into a corner of the camera bag, then strapped the bag over the horn of the old saddle. "You know," she said, "I did go back to the stables to see if they had some boots I could wear, but there wasn't anything in my size—one of the disadvantages of tiny feet. But I think these scarves will do nicely."

Brad took the reins of the black and mounted expertly. "Whoa! Easy, easy," he called out, holding the reins in one hand and stroking the skittish horse's neck with the other, until the high-strung animal stopped its snorting and head-shaking.

While Terry got ready, Brad walked the stallion around in a little half-circle. When Terry paused to pull up one of the wide shoulder straps of her dress, Brad pointed to it and asked, "Are you really planning to ride like that? They'll be talking about us around here for *another* seven years. . . ."

Terry laughed. "Never fear, modesty will prevail," she said, taking a large safety pin from the pocket of her sundress. Not entirely unaware of the effect this would have on Brad, she leaned over, reached down between her knees and took hold of the back hem of the dress. Matching it to the corresponding part of the front hem and gathering the two together in a bunch, she fastened them together with the safety pin.

"Voilà," she said, straightening up and stretching her arms out. "Instant riding culottes!"

"Marvelous!" Brad called, pulling back on the reins and letting his horse rear. He laughed with pleasure. "That's the resourceful Terry I remember!"

Terry laughed back, full of the moment's high good humor. Taking the bay's reins from the bemused saddleboy and putting her left hand on the horn and her left bare foot into the silk-covered stirrup, she mounted in one quick motion. "Giddap," she said, brushing her bare heels against the flanks of the horse.

And, still joking and laughing, she and Brad cantered away, riding side by side toward the lake shore.

They rode through the warm, golden May afternoon, talking and reminiscing, stopping to take photographs and record scraps of narrative for their book. As they rode out of an area of evergreen and broadleafed woods, out onto a bare and wind-swept bluff high above the beach, Terry felt exquisitely, totally alive; the cold air blowing in from the huge sea-lake swept her hair back from her sculpted face and seemed to open every pore and invigorate every cell of her body.

"Whoa!" She pulled the bay up short, stopping to fit a wide-angle lens to her camera. "I'm going to get a shot of this panorama," she called out to Brad, who turned the black around and came back beside her. "How magnificent!" she said. "Just look at it!"

To the horizon and beyond, much farther than the eye could see, shone sparkling, white-flecked Lake Superior, the marine blue of its water melding into the cerulean of the cloudless sky.

"By the shores of Gitche Gumee," Brad murmured. He cocked a brow. "Remember your fourth-grade poetry?"

"Hm-m," she responded, distracted by the sight before her.

"Longfellow. *The Song of Hiawatha.* You know, 'By the shores of Gitche Gumee, By the shining Big-Sea-Water . . .

"This is the place," Brad continued. "Lake Superior is what Longfellow had in mind when he wrote about the shining shore of the Big-Sea-Water."

"Really?"

"Really."

Terry put her camera away. "Impressive—and poetic," she said.

Brad replied with more earnest feeling than she had expected, "Ever since we got here, I've been feeling sentimental; snatches of old songs, seem to rise to my lips. I keep remembering lines I learned in school, like 'the end of all our exploring/Will be to come back to where we began/And know it as if for the first time.' Appropriate—for us, I mean—isn't it?"

He was serious, Terry knew, but she wasn't ready to be. "My, how did you ever get to be so knowledgeable?" she teased. "If I didn't know better I'd say you spent all your time in college with your nose in a book."

Brad laughed, too, responding to her bantering tone. "Oh, there's nothing to it," he said with exaggerated modesty. "It's easy, in fact; all you need is a razor sharp mind and the services of the fifty-person news research department at the network."

"So that's how you do it," Terry said with amusement, reining in the bay.

"Told you it was easy," Brad replied. "C'mon, let's find a way down to the shoreline," he added, turning the black's head sharply. He and the stallion shot away, galloping along the bluff. Still grinning to herself, Terry followed after.

They had dismounted and were walking side by side ahead of their horses along the narrow, pebble-strewn beach, far beneath the gray and pink-streaked granite cliffs. Occasionally, Terry stopped to pick up a greenstone or a particularly delicate shell.

"This one would make a nice necklace or a ring," she said, showing Brad a tiny deep green chip in her palm. As she had done with the other stones and shells, she handed it to him and he put it into one of the deep pockets of his jodhpurs.

"The color reminds me of how the water looked the other time we were here; you know, that winter-green color like aquamarine."

Again, Terry was impressed by Brad's poetic, but accurate, recollections. "That's right, when we came down here everything was covered with snow, except the lake, and we saw that black bear and those otters sliding down a snowbank. . . ."

"And I brought along the down sleeping bag," Brad added quietly, not having to remind Terry of what had happened next, of how they had made love—wild, passionate love—on the sleeping bag stretched out under a pine tree near the shore. They had been two kids then—unashamed of their love or their sensuality—two kids alone in nature on a cold December day, making love underneath a gray sky while emerald green waves, tipped by sprays of white foam, crashed to the icy shore nearby. But that was then. . . .

And this was now. With a deep breath Terry shook free of the enchantment that, with the memory, had taken hold of her.

"That was a long time ago," she whispered, not daring to look at Brad. She reached over to retrieve another greenstone from the ground. "This would make a good ring, too," she said, handing it to Brad.

"Keep looking," Brad said, "and you might even find a diamond."

"A diamond?" Terry jumped at the opportunity to draw him out on a less pointed subject. "You're kidding, of course."

"Well, it is highly unlikely," Brad admitted, "but not at all impossible. It's the glaciers, you see, the same ones that formed Lake Superior in the first place, many thousands of years ago. The glaciers deposited all kinds of odd things in the strangest places. Like diamonds, for instance.

"Every few years, some lucky fool in some place like Ohio—or Michigan—will be tramping through a bog, or a swamp, or just over a patch of rocks, and there will be a high grade diamond—sometimes a big one, too, worth quite a lot—sitting there. And that diamond was carried down by the ice during the Ice Age. Geologists figure quite a few were dropped around Lake Superior, both around here and on the north shore, even though none have been reported for years. So, who knows, this might be our lucky day."

For a few minutes, as they continued to walk ahead of the horses, Terry studied the beach with renewed interest, but no sparkling diamond appeared at her feet. At last, they came to a place where the high bluffs curled down to meet the water and their path along the shore was blocked. Squawking seagulls flew overhead.

"Looks like we'll have to retrace our path," Brad said jauntily.

"Let's ride back."

"Good idea. But there's no hurry, is there? There's still plenty of light. Why don't we have lunch here? It looks like a nice, quiet spot. You can take some more photographs if you want."

"Okay," Terry agreed. "These rock formations

meeting the water will make a good composition, and there are plenty of gulls and shore birds to snap."

"Right." Brad pointed up to a shadowy niche just below the crest of one of the bluffs. "That might even be an eagle's nest," he observed, pulling the saddle bags down from her horse's saddle, then tethering it and the bay to a nearby stump. He reached into the bags, pulled out a small cooler and a large beach blanket, which he spread out just above the tideline.

Terry sank down gratefully onto the blanket. "Whew, I'm really tired," she said with some surprise. "I had no idea until just now. I guess I can use a few minutes of rest."

"Sure, why not? We've been going practically non-stop for days." Brad knelt on the blanket. He put the bags and the cooler between them and began to empty out their contents. "I don't know about you, but I'm not only tired, I'm hungry—and thirsty, too," he added, extracting a cold bottle of Chablis from the cooler and opening it. "Oh, and don't worry, I don't expect you to join me this time if you don't want to; after all, this is supposed to be a vacation for *me,* but not for you. I guess I finally realized that after our little canoe fiasco yesterday."

As Brad said this, Terry felt stirrings of guilt—and something else. She picked up one of the two wine glasses that he had set out between them and word-lessly held it out for him to fill. "This can't have been much of a vacation for you so far," she said quietly, feeling a little sad. Brad filled her glass. "I guess I haven't made it easy for you either," she admitted, "always reminding you that I'm only along for busi-ness-business-business. I could use some vacation myself, a break from the everyday chores and responsibilities. . . ."

"Well, you'll never have a better opportunity than right now," Brad remarked, gazing out at the vista of sea and sky before them. "A seashore, solitude, Chablis . . . Oh yes, and good food—I had Mrs. Klaus pack us one of her special lunches."

"Excellent," Terry agreed, her mouth watering at the thought of Mrs. Klaus's culinary delights. She was finding it easier and easier to get into the spirit of the lazy Spring afternoon. "A toast then," she said, holding up her glass. "To our book and to this day of playing hooky from the real world."

Brad smiled at her earnest offering. "To you," he said simply, looking deep into her eyes.

Terry responded playfully. "And to you," she added.

"To *us,*" Brad amended, clinking her glass and drinking before she could object.

For the moment wide-eyed and alert, Terry listened and sipped the Chablis, while Brad unwrapped dishes and catalogued their menu in his deep announcer's voice. "Two salads—one green and some sort of Greek-looking dish with cucumbers and olives and lots of lemons on the side. Too bad we don't have any Ouzo. Cold, steamed vegetables in a sesame dressing, I think; cold broiled chicken—just smell that marinade! Some kind of flaky pastry thing—I can't even begin to guess what it's filled with; and, my favorites, pecan brownies! Lord, they're going to have to get a crane to lift us out of here after this meal!"

Terry laughed and sipped her wine. "I'll just take

a bit of everything—except for those pastry things, of course. I want *two* of those. . . ."

Like the weather and the horseback ride and the secluded location itself, the picnic meal was superb!

"Quite a floor show," Brad remarked, nodding in the direction of the black and white shore birds that were chasing each other up and down the sand. He offered Terry part of the last of the wine, but she declined with a sleepy little shake of her head, so he poured it for himself. "Aren't you going to get a shot of those sandpipers?" he asked.

"Maybe later," Terry said softly. She stretched out on her back on the blanket, pulling the hem of her sundress several inches above her knees. "I think I'll just lie here and get some of this warm afternoon sun. . . . Anyway, those are plovers, not sandpipers."

"Really?" Brad stood up and walked behind her. "How can you tell?"

"The sandpipers are a shade lighter. . . ." As she stared up at the sky, Terry saw, just out of the corner of her eye, one of Brad's expensive knee-high riding boots go sailing through the air and land in front of the beach towel.

"Do go on," his mellifluous voice said from somewhere just behind her.

"And, uh, the sandpipers have these vertical stripes running all up and down their front. . . ." Another boot flew through the air. "But the plovers, like the killdeer and such, usually only have one or two horizontal stripes along the tops of their otherwise white breasts, so, you see, these little birds—" Terry stopped abruptly as the dark brown jodhpurs landed next to the two boots. "Bradford Andrews, *what* do you think you're doing?" she asked, not daring to turn her head.

"Don't worry." Terry saw a flash of red and tan. "I have my swimming suit on underneath my riding duds. I was just changing, that's all, so I could get a little sun, too. I hope you don't mind." Terry peeked over at Brad, who was now sitting on the other side of the blanket. He was wearing red boxer trunks, and as she watched he pulled off his tan polo shirt and stretched out on his back. "Ahh, that's great," he sighed. "Cold wine, warm sun . . . just wonderful."

Quickly Terry closed her eyes, but she was unable to erase the image of his body—the hard-muscled legs and the torso still trim. Aware of the flush on her cheek, she turned her face to the side, away from Brad, and took several measured deep breaths. Gradually, she was able to grow calm. Finally, she slept.

Although she dozed on warm sand and it was a brilliant, sunny Spring afternoon, in Terry's dream it was that long-ago winter day again and she was once more wrapped in Brad's arms. In her dream they became the playful otters they had once seen, frolicking in the snow, and Brad was nuzzling her cheek. *How it tickled. . . .*

"Wake up, sleepy head."

Terry came to with a start. Brad was kneeling beside her, his hand outstretched, gently shaking her shoulder.

"What's so funny?" he asked.

"What?" She put her hand up, palm out, above her forehead, to shield her eyes from the sun.

Brad smiled down at her and chuckled. "I've been listening to you giggling in your sleep for the last ten minutes," he said. "You seemed to be having such a good timc, I couldn't stand it anymore. Anyway, that sun is strong enough to burn and you've been in one position too long. Turn over and I'll put some of this suntan oil on your back."

"Okay," Terry agreed sleepily. She rolled over on her stomach. She heard the sucking sound that the plastic bottle made when Brad squeezed the tanning oil into his palm and smelled the heady aroma of cocoa butter.

"Just a sec'," she said, reaching around behind her back to unfasten the top three buttons of her dress. "No use wasting all that good sun just to get a tanning line across the middle of my shoulder blades," she added.

"And beautiful shoulder blades they are, too," Brad observed, gently sliding the straps off her shoulders and separating the two sides, so that her back was bare all the way to her slim waist. "And no bra strap, either," he remarked.

Terry's face was turned to the side and covered by her blond hair, so Brad couldn't see that she smiled to herself. "Silly, sometimes I wonder about you—Mr. Observant Newsman, indeed!

"OOOH!" Terry arched her back and shivered as the cold tanning oil fell on the small of her back. "Watch it!"

"Serves you right," Brad said, his breathy whisper belying the lightness of his words. His strong hands began to work their way up her spinal cord all the way to her long neck, then started to knead the muscles of her shoulders. "Aahh," he sighed, as if it were he being massaged and not the other way around. "Sometimes I wonder about you, too," he mused, his powerful hands working their way back down the muscles over her rib cage, then threading their way lightly up her spine again. "I wonder and I wonder; you *are* a wonder—a natural wonder—more beautiful than anything I've ever seen."

His hands stroked her neck, her shoulders, ran playfully up and down her spine. "I'll do your legs," he said, not waiting for an answer to put the cooling oil on her taut calf muscles.

She should have protested; she should have jumped up and reminded him of his status as an engaged man, of how they were only there on business, of how his hands were gliding over areas where the sun wouldn't shine.

But she didn't. They were alone, on a deserted beach, far from society and its constraints, far from any demands but those of their own desires.

The promise was forgotten! Terry heard no warning voices. There was only the pounding of the waves and the roaring of the blood as it rushed through her veins. . . .

"Roll over, I'll do your front." She responded to his husky urgent whisper without a word, even helping when Brad pulled off her dress.

His hands ran up and down her torso and circled her breasts, leaving traces of cold fire wherever they went.

Terry moaned, shivering with pleasure, as Brad's hands pulled at her flimsy bikini briefs.

Suddenly they, too, were gone, and her back was arched and her hands were reaching out to encircle Brad's head and he was raining kisses down on her eyes, her mouth, her neck. . . .

She burned with primitive desire and overwhelming need as his mouth moved toward her breasts, firm and swollen with desire. She moaned, burning with pleasure as his tongue first traced the curve of her breasts, then moved down her straining, aching, churning body.

Biting her lip to keep from crying out, she ran her hands through his hair and over his face, while his kisses and the butterfly touch of his breath moved rhythmically back up her arched torso.

Once again, he paused to kiss each breast, then buried his face in the hollow of her neck. His hands ran down the front of her body, enflaming her excruciatingly sensitive skin wherever they touched.

He kissed her cheeks, her chin, her eyes. His hungry mouth found hers and the full length of his body pressed ardently against her. His scent mixed with the aroma of tanning oil and the brackish sea smells wafting in from the lake. Deliriously she dug her hands into his back, urging him on to an ever-greater frenzy.

Over and over he whispered her name. Her cries of pleasure were lost amid the crashing of the waves and the raucous calls of the gulls patroling the shores. Behind them, at the height of their ecstasy, the black stallion reared, whinnied, and stamped its hooves. . . .

Waves of pleasure receded like the tide. When Terry opened her eyes and looked up, a Golden eagle—its graceful body dark except for the white tips of its magnificently outstretched wings—wheeled in the patch of blue sky above them.

For a time they rested in each others' arms. Then, as the afternoon shadows lengthened, they slowly dressed and packed, working together with unspoken, but mutual, understanding.

They mounted their horses and raced off, galloping back along the shore at full speed. It was as if, Terry decided later, they thought that by hurrying back they might bring some of the magic with them and, perhaps, make this impossible moment last just a bit longer.

"I make how you like it, yes?"

"Superb," Terry agreed, taking a sip from the long-stemmed martini glass that Mrs. Klaus had set on the table in the center of the small dimly lighted dining room. "Very dry."

"Ganz gut," the ruddy-faced woman said, drying her thick peasant's hands on the front of her apron. "See, I not forget."

Terry smiled. "And it's been such a long time." She had agreed to meet Brad for a special dinner that Frau Klaus had promised them as soon as they had arrived back at the lodge. After showering and changing into a simple, but classic, black cocktail dress, she had come downstairs. Now, as she looked around the small dining room with the crackling fireplace she remembered so well, Terry noticed that none of the other tables was prepared for diners; they were all covered with linen, but the one at which she sat was the only one with silverware, lighted candles and a spray of cut flowers. "But where's everyone else?" she asked. "I remember that your little dining room was always jam-packed."

"Ach!" Mrs. Klaus waved her hand in a characteristic dismissive gesture. "Vee not even open, Albrecht and me, not until after this—how you say *Denkmal Tag?*"

"Memorial Day?" Terry ventured.

"*Ja,* Memory day. No, *nein, nein,*" she said emphatically, "vee not vonce open until dis jahr." She leaned over and whispered conspiratorially to Terry. "Vee vatch your junge man on television, and do you know vot he do?"

"No, what?" Terry whispered back. In the hallway, behind Frau Klaus, Terry saw Brad as he bounded down the last two steps of the stairs and ran over to a small mahogany desk where white-haired, bespectacled Herr Klaus sat. Quickly, Brad made a phone call; then, just as quickly, he reached into his pocket and handed something to Mr. Klaus, who nodded over and over again, as if commiting a complicated set of instructions to memory. Then he, too, got on the telephone, while Brad slowly, deliberately walked back toward the dining room.

Mrs. Klaus leaned down and whispered into Terry's ear. "He call up. He say, 'du *must* open!' He say, 'I pay for alle *twanzig* rooms.'"

Terry gave her a quizzical look as Brad approached nearer. "You're sure?" she asked. "He paid for *all* twenty rooms, just so you'd open the lodge a week early?"

Frau Klaus straightened up and nodded sagely. "*Ja,* naturlich. He hast great *liebe* fur you, *ja.*" And, seeing Brad just behind her, she giggled and skittered away, back to her kitchen.

Terry had expected to see Brad in slacks and a sweater or perhaps a sports jacket. Remembering how, this time, the door between their adjoining rooms had been left open, and how she'd listened to his off-key singing in the shower, brought a small smile to her lips. But the smile died as soon as she took in what he was wearing and saw what he had in his hand.

He had on his flying clothes again, his jeans and boots and the crinkly leather jacket, and in his hand was his suitcase.

Brad's other hand was clenched into a fist. Slowly he opened it in front of her to reveal the crumpled, damp-looking slip of blue paper he was clutching.

"After I showered," Brad began in a tight, almost choked voice. "I unpacked my wet clothes—you know, the ones I wore canoeing. Back in Minneapolis, I just threw them into the suitcase without looking, without bothering to check. . . .

"The shirt I was wearing, the madras," he continued in the same, strangely disassociated voice, "was bleeding all over my other clothes, so I got ready to throw it away. Only first I checked the pockets. . . ."

Brad swallowed hard, then resumed. "There were the notes, the ones that Rick, that chauffeur kid, brought, the ones I never looked at. They were all nothing, just the usual odds and ends, except for one. . . . This one."

He dropped the note on the table. "I must leave—*now,*" he said in a voice that brooked no challenge. "I'm flying to Detroit—*tonight*. They're holding a commercial plane there for me so I can make New York before morning."

Terry felt all the color drain from her face. She felt as if a cold wind had swept in from the north, killing every last sign of the verdant Spring. "But why?" she managed to ask at last. "What is it?"

Brad shook his head, his clenched jaw set in a hard line. "I can't say," he said tersely through lips that barely moved. "You'll have to trust me. I've made arrangements with Mr. Klaus; I've left money so you'll be able to get back to Chicago. Please, just trust me for a little while. . . ."

"Trust you?" Terry wanted to sound hard, bitter even, but above all in control. Instead what came out was a screech of betrayal. She gripped the martini glass tightly in one hand. "After *this?* After doing this to me *here, again.* It's a nightmare!"

She stood up, heedlessly knocking back her chair, within a hair's breath of throwing her drink in Brad's face. "It's a goddamn nightmare!" she screamed. And then she lost all semblance of control and she *did* throw the drink into his face—she threw it hard, as hard as she could!

"Get out!" she said in a cold fury. "I never want to see you again. I don't give a damn what your reason is for this, I don't care what piece of business it is that you find so important. . . ."

Brad backed away from her.

"Go on, leave! Just go!"

For a second, he looked undecided. "I really can't explain," he mumbled in a distraught voice. "They'll only hold the Detroit flight so long. . . ."

"Get out!" she spat, looking around for something else to throw. "I hope you got your twenty rooms worth, you bastard!"

Brad flinched. "I'm sorry," he whispered. Then he turned on his heel and was gone.

For a full minute Terry just stood there, as if in shock, staring at the empty space where he had been. Then at last, rousing herself from the recurring nightmare, trying not to recall how this had all happened to her here once before, she looked down at the table and saw there the crumpled slip of blue paper. Slowly she unfolded it and read the single cryptic sentence that was written there: *"Urgent you call C. in N.Y. immediately,"* the note read.

The words swam before her eyes: "*. . . C. in N.Y. . . .*" The paper fluttered to the floor; Terry's hand went to her throat and she gasped as if she could feel the knife twisting in her back.

chapter

6

TERRY FELT HUMILIATED, but her friend Millie Foster was the only one to whom she would say so.

It was the afternoon of the day following the scene with Brad in the dining room of the Paradise Lodge, and she was back in her cozy apartment on the top floor of Millie's comfortable North Chicago house. As Terry unpacked, she told Millie about her adventures (and misadventures) of the past several days. Millie, whose passion for juicy gossip equalled her love of good food, was listening avidly.

"You know, Millie, it was just crazy—the whole idea behind the trip was crazy. I was supposed to photograph the nature spots in the Midwest that were 'meaningful' to this 'famous person,' meaningful to

Brad. I was skeptical all along, and I was right to be."

"Why?" Millie asked. "It seemed like a big chance for you, didn't it? I mean, a big chance in more ways than one."

Terry hung up her cameras in her combination closet/darkroom and turned back to her friend. "It was a big chance, all right," she said ruefully, "but it was that no-good Brad's chance, not mine."

"But why?"

"Because these 'meaningful places' he picked out were the very places we went to as young lovers in college, young lovers who used any excuse—a botany field trip, a visit to a nature preserve, a 'sick' relative—to get away and be alone together. And that cad knew that if we zigzagged all around the countryside to these same romantic places in the same damn order as before he could seduce the naive Midwestern girl, who was still pining for him after all these years, seduce *me* with my own memories! Mr. Big Shot TV Star, indeed," she added bitterly.

Millie leaned forward eagerly. "And did he?" she asked.

Terry put away the last of her things and flopped down on her bed. "Did he what?" she asked, absentmindedly brushing a strand of hair away from her face.

"Seduce you, of course."

"Millie!"

"Come on, we're friends, you can tell me. . . ."

Terry smiled enigmatically. "*Ladies* don't kiss and tell *either,* not even to their best friends."

Brad was by far the most ardent lover she had ever known, or could even imagine knowing. And with the passage of years he had acquired spectacular techniques to complement his spectacular passion. Terry smiled to herself: despite how it had ended, she would always have the memory of that one afternoon of matchless, exquisite, ecstatic passion at the water's edge. "Brad Andrews is a bastard," she said in an affectionate, wistful whisper that answered Millie's question. "A real Grade A, Number One bastard!"

"We've got to do something!" Millie said emphatically, rousing Terry from her romantic reverie. "We can't just let this be the end. . . ."

"Oh, Millie, it *is* the end," Terry replied with finality. She felt a great sadness welling up in her.

"But—"

"Shh." Terry's finger at her lips silenced her friend's well-meaning protest. "No," she added softly, "it's all over. It was all over several years ago. And," she added on a cry of pain, "it should have *stayed* 'over'!"

For a full minute the two friends sat in total silence. Millie chewed thoughtfully on her lower lip, her wide, freckled forehead furrowed. She looked as if she was desperate to come up with a way to bring Brad and Terry back together, to find some way to erase events that could never be undone. Terry sat primly on the edge of her bed, her legs crossed at the ankles, her knees together, her small hands folded in her lap. She stared straight ahead, her calm demeanor offering no clue to the jumble of thoughts and memories in her mind. Then, breaking the silence, the front-door bell rang downstairs.

Millie jumped up and hurried to answer it, while Terry got up and began rummaging around in her desk, looking for a pencil and a piece of paper. *Got to pull myself together,* she thought, *got to get busy and make a list of what I have to do.*

She had gotten as far as the first three items—1. *Process exposed rolls of film.* 2. *Send proof sheets to S. McMasters.* 3. *Go to dry cleaners.*—when Millie burst through the door.

"There's someone here to see you," she announced breathlessly.

"Who?" Terry asked suspiciously, suddenly fearing that it might be Brad.

"She won't say. An elderly woman, very elegant. She looks like a duchess or something. She says you know her."

Terry was puzzled. "Tell her I'll be right down, will you please?"

"Sure, I'll make some tea," Millie said, turning to leave.

"A duchess," Terry repeated to herself as soon as Millie was gone. She glanced at herself in the mirror over the dresser, wondering if she should change into something more appropriate for meeting visiting royalty. *No,* she decided, giving her mirror-image an ironic little smile. Comfortable white pleated pants with gray piping and a plum-colored, collarless, baggy, Russian peasant blouse made quite a respectable outfit in which to be seen by anyone—even a duchess! She slipped her bare feet into her old espadrilles and marched down the stairs, the very picture of the confident, modern woman, but she wasn't prepared for the surprise that awaited her in the downstairs sitting room.

Millie had been right to call the old woman seated in the Queen Anne wing chair on the other side of the room a "duchess"; it was, in fact, very close to the private name that Terry had always used for this aristocratic old woman, who was still dressed all in black, in an old-fashioned, high-necked dress, and who still wore her gray hair in a meticulously done, swept-back chignon. To Terry, she had been the Dowager Empress then; the passage of time had done nothing to alter the appropriateness of the name. She still looked every inch the queen.

"Hello, Theresa," the old woman said, in the same high, but firm voice. "So nice to see you again after all these years." Regally, she held out her frail hand.

Terry stepped forward and shook it lightly, resisting the impossible little-girl impulse to curtsey as she did so. "Hello, Mrs. Andrews," she replied deferentially. "This is quite a surprise."

"I was on my way to California," Brad's mother explained, "and decided to stop in Chicago to visit with you for a few minutes. It was an impulse. I thought it was past time that we had a talk. Don't you agree, Theresa?"

"Yes . . . yes, I suppose I do." *'On impulse,'* Terry repeated to herself. *Since when does the Dowager Empress do anything on impulse?*

Millie came into the room just then, carrying her best silver tea service. Terry welcomed the opportunity to introduce Millie to Brad's mother, but her respite was all too brief; as soon as Millie heard who Terry's visitor was, she disappeared from the room.

"Tea, Mrs. Andrews?" Terry asked politely, as soon as Millie was gone.

"Yes, thank you, Theresa," the Dowager Empress said in her reedy voice.

"Do you still take a little milk and no sugar?"

"Why, yes, how charming of you to remember," the old woman said, seeming genuinely surprised. "Thank you, Theresa." She took the blue and white china cup that Terry brought over to her.

Terry sat down on the faded Chippendale sofa across the room and poured tea for herself. She was surprised to see that, in contrast to the old woman, *her* hands were shaking. "Mrs. Andrews, I was wondering," she began respectfully. "My friend Millie said you wouldn't give your name. . . ."

The old woman smiled. "And you were wondering why, you thought it was 'out of character' for me, is that so, my dear?"

"Yes, I suppose so." Terry was glad that the old woman had finished her awkward question for her and was taking it seriously.

Again the old woman smiled. "It's very simple, Theresa; if you weren't so good-hearted and didn't have such a high opinion of my—shall we call it my 'fortitude'?—you would know the answer right away."

Terry gave her a puzzled look. "I'm afraid I still don't understand."

For a third time the old woman smiled indulgently. "Why, I was afraid you would refuse to see me, of course," she said. "And I have to admit to you that I've come to think that you have good cause."

Terry was shocked by this admission. A part of her had always understood the actions that Brad's mother had once taken. "You acted like a mother protecting her son," Terry stated with conviction. "You only did what you thought was right. I never held *that* against you."

Something in the old woman's granite features

seemed to soften. "I was right to come here," she said with feeling, a triumphant note in her high-pitched voice, as if a longtime argument in her mind had just been settled once and for all. "I was right to review my actions and to reconsider what I had done."

"But—"

"Please, Theresa, let me continue. Let me apologize to you. I want to explain to you what I did and why. I want to get it off my chest. It's something that's been bothering me for a long, long time. . . ."

Carefully, the Dowager Empress put down her tea cup and saucer on the small pedestal table next to her chair. "I thought your affair would prevent the success that I foresaw Bradford would have," she began. "I thought you were the wrong girl for him, from the wrong background. I was wrong," she said succinctly.

"You know that when he came to me and declared that you were to be married, I opposed it. You know that I said he would be disinherited and I would never speak to him again.

"You may even know that Bradford was ready to risk his inheritance and my affections—all for you. What you do not know is what I did as soon as he left the room to return to you. I called an old friend in New York—an old suitor, actually, whom I had once rejected in favor of Bradford's father—and I requested a favor, a favor which Dr. Stanfield was only too happy to provide. . . ."

"Dr. Stanfield!"

"Yes," the old woman confirmed, looking down and shaking her head in sorrow. "Bradford never knew that the Chairman of the Board of the company that owned the network was my dear friend. Bradford never suspected that the offer of employment in the very position he'd dreamed about for half his life—the offer to be a network foreign correspondent; the offer with an ironclad time limitation for his acceptance and with the single stipulation that he be unmarried—came to him because of me."

"He thought the rule about being single was because it was a dangerous assignment," Terry interjected in amazement.

"I know," the old woman said. "The dangerous assignments came later, it's true, but the first assignment was to a vacation spot, a resort area in France where I thought he would meet eligible young women of his own position in society. . . ."

"'Eligible young women?'" Terry repeated, as if in a trance.

"Oh, I know how it must sound to you," the old woman said contritely. "I was deluded then.

"As the years went by, mutual friends—as friends will—kept me posted on some of the events of your life. I learned how you left school to care for your parents when they became ill and how you stayed with them through the end. I learned how you resumed your studies, how you worked to support yourself and how, finally, you attained advanced degrees and began to accumulate honors in your chosen field. . . ."

"But, Mrs. Andrews—"

"No, Theresa, let me finish. They say old people, like old dogs, cannot learn new tricks. Rubbish! Only ignorant people cannot learn. I tell you again, I was wrong," the old woman said emphatically. She lifted her head proudly; her eyes glistening, she looked directly into Terry's face. "I should have been more confident, more trusting. I should have seen that nothing could prevent Bradford's success; it was ordained. But his personal happiness was not. And this is what I have prevented by breaking up your relationship. Can you ever forgive me, can you ever forgive an old woman who wants nothing more than to attend her son's wedding?"

Terry swallowed hard. "Mrs. Andrews, I *do* forgive you. I forgave you long ago. But, but—there must be some mistake. . . ."

The old woman smiled joyfully. "Mistake? What possible mistake . . ."

"Brad and I aren't getting married. In fact, I don't expect I'll ever see him again."

"What? But—" For the first time since Terry had met her, Brad's mother appeared confused.

"Brad's getting married all right, Mrs. Andrews, but not to me."

"What?" the old woman repeated. "Who?"

"Caroline McMasters," Terry said simply.

"Her?" The Dowager Empress seemed to be in complete shock. "But—but I thought my son's purpose in returning to Chicago was to win your hand?"

What Terry said then made her realize later that she had never really forgiven the old woman; a part of her still wanted to cause the Dowager Empress pain.

"It wasn't my *hand* that Brad was interested in winning," she observed dryly.

All the color drained from Mrs. Andrews's face. "I'm terribly sorry to intrude on you like this," she said. "You must think I'm a terrible old fool. Please forgive me; no, don't get up. I have a cab waiting for me outside." And in a moment the Dowager Empress Andrews was gone.

Terry felt terrible, but whether it was for poor Mrs. Andrews or for herself she couldn't say. Slowly she walked to the front window and peeked outside. As Brad's mother rushed down the front walk and into the waiting taxicab, she passed the mailman who was about to make the day's delivery.

Although Terry didn't know it, worse was yet to come.

chapter 7

IT WAS A SUMMONS, not a request—a coldly formal note—but Terry had no choice except to honor it. So she stayed up most of the night developing film and making proof sheets to bring to a luncheon meeting with the McMasterses.

Then the next morning she dressed in her purple gabardine blazer, matching trousers, and cranberry crepe de chine blouse, borrowed Millie's old Chevy and drove down to the Loop. In her big, black leather shoulder bag, in addition to the freshly dried proof sheets, was the new Leica that Brad had bought her.

Terry knew the restaurant where the meeting had been scheduled. It was dark, wood paneled and private, with a small menu and a large, well-stocked bar.

Recently, to honor the huge outdoor sculptures facing each other across the plaza outside and to garner a little publicity, the restaurant's shrewd new owner had renamed the little place The Two Women.

As she had hoped, Terry arrived a few minutes early, so she used the extra time to wander around the mid-Loop plaza, snapping the Miró and Picasso sculptures from various angles and listening to the comments of tourists and office workers out on their lunch hours, comments like, "What the hell is that?" and "I haven't the vaguest idea what it's supposed to be but I kinda like the way it looks." As Terry had expected, the process of composing photographs of the abstract woman's head by Picasso and the forty-foot-high womanlike figure called "Miró's Chicago" helped her to compose herself. By the time she stepped into the cool dark entrance of the restaurant, she was more than ready to do business with Sarah and her husband Caroll, but no amount of preparation could have prepared her for who they had with them.

She was taller than Terry would have guessed and dressed all in yellow, her clear skin and pretty features marred by a sullen, almost morose, expression. What color her shoulder-length hair had been originally was impossible to guess; at the moment it was silver, and the straight line of bangs across her forehead, as well as the Prince Valiant hairdo itself, added to a first impression of a silvery, metallic, armored helmet on the young woman's head.

"Hello, Miss Rovik, how nice to see you again," bow-tied Caroll McMasters said genially as soon as Terry arrived at the booth in the corner of the restaurant. "I'd like to introduce our darling daughter Caroline."

"Hello."

"Hullo," the young, silver-haired woman said, just barely glancing at Terry as she listlessly shook her hand.

"Hello, Sarah."

"Hello . . . *dear,*" replied Sarah, her greeting showing even less enthusiasm, but distinctly more animosity, than that of her sulky daughter. She fitted a brown cigarette into her onyx and gold holder. While she lighted it, Terry had a chance to take in the way Sarah looked: there were bags under her sharp eyes, thin lines at the corners of her mouth and her wiry black hair definitely seemed streaked by more gray. To Terry's observant photographer's eyes it was obvious that Sarah McMasters had been having a hard time since their last meeting, and she wondered how much it had to do with her and with daughter Caroline's presence at this so-called "business lunch."

From the way everyone ordered salads and then just barely nibbled at them, it was obvious that no one was there for the food.

"Shall we begin?" Sarah said at last, when the after-lunch coffee and drinks had arrived. She exhaled a thin stream of smoke. "Pass the sugar, dear," she added to her daughter.

Terry reached into her bag and pulled out the proof sheets of the photographs she'd taken on the trip with Brad. "Here are the first contact sheets. I circled some of the best shots. I think you'll like them, they're just what we talked about before."

"Oh good," Caroll said enthusiastically.

Sarah took the sheets, barely glanced at them, then passed them on to her husband, who carefully studied each shot.

"Well then, dear, has everything been satisfactory for you thus far?" Sarah asked, as she used a long, ruby fingernail to slit open the flaps of two packets of sugar. "We do like to keep our artists happy, and we do like them to inform us whenever they have any—shall we say, 'difficult encounters'?"

"No, no problems," Terry replied with an upbeat little smile. She reached into her bag, dug out her Bausch & Lomb magnifying glass and handed it to Caroll, saying, "Those contact-sheet frames are a little hard to see without one of these."

"Oh, thank you, Miss Rovik. . . ."

"Please call me 'Terry'. . . ."

"Oh, yes, this is much better—Terry," Caroll said emphatically. He peered intently through the magnifying glass. "Oh, I do like this one, this funny little animal face."

"That's an owl we found inside a tree on a tiny island in the middle of a river in Minnesota. Brad said—"

"Yes, *Brad,*" Sarah cut in, using the clinking sound her spoon made against the sides of the cup as she stirred her coffee to draw Terry's attention back. "Do tell us how you found working with dear Brad. I hope you weren't put off by all those women who are forever asking him for autographs and following him around. What was that you called them once, dear?" she asked her daughter.

Caroline put down her glass of chilled white wine. "You mean 'groupies', Mother?" she asked, her tone plainly exasperated.

"Yes, that's it." Sarah turned back to Terry. "And were you bothered by these 'groupie' women?"

Terry dunked her tea bag several times while she answered. "Oh, no . . . not at all . . . Brad seems to handle his admirers quite well. . . . He's had—a lot of practice." She put the bag on the saucer and took a sip of hot tea that scalded her mouth.

"Yes, isn't that just what you were saying, dear?" Again Sarah addressed her daughter. "Didn't you tell me how urbanely Brad dealt with that woman who was rude enough to bother you in the World Trade Center?"

"Yes, Mother," Caroline replied in the same voice as before.

Sarah took a drink of the sweet black coffee and another deep drag from her cigarette. Her gimlet eyes watched Terry carefully. "Caroline and Brad had the most *wonderful* reunion last night in New York," she said in a rheumy whisper. "They went to a *wonderful, romantic* restaurant on top of the World Trade Center, where you can see absolutely all of the city. What was that called, dear?" she asked Caroline.

"The Windows on the World, Mother."

"Yes, Windows on the World," Sarah repeated, her voice seeming to caress the words and mingle them with her hissing exhale of another stream of thick cigarette smoke.

"How nice," Terry observed mildly, hoping that it didn't sound too forced.

"Then spending all that time in the company of a handsome, famous, cosmopolite didn't make you too—shall we say, 'uncomfortable'? Didn't intrude on your work?"

Terry's steady demeanor faltered just a bit. "I was able to do my job," she retorted curtly. "If you have any questions about the photographs, I'll be glad to answer them."

"Not at all, dear," Sarah replied smoothly. "I have complete confidence in your *artistic* sensibility. . . ."

For a fraction of a second, Sarah's implied criticism hung in the air—like her cigarette smoke it was a pall between them—before Caroline asked abruptly, "Have you got any change, Mother? I want to make a phone call."

"Don't you have a dime yourself, dear?" Sarah asked back sweetly, still not taking her eyes away from Terry.

"I need quarters. Lots of them. I want to call long distance."

"Ask your father, dear, to give you a few dollar bills, then get change from the barman," Sarah instructed patronizingly. Terry was aghast. Sarah was talking to Caroline, who was probably in her mid-twenties, as if she were a five-year-old child. *This* was the woman Brad intended to marry? How *could* he?

But when tall, graceful Caroline stood up and sashayed away, her petulant look replaced by an impassive public expression, every male head in the dark restaurant-bar turned to follow her undulant progress. *That explains it,* Terry thought ruefully, *sexy blondes, even pseudo-blondes, always were Brad's type—plus she's the "proper" social class for someone of his eminence.*

The thought that this sullen child-woman was probably going off to phone Brad in New York infuriated Terry, but she said nothing. She just sat there with a small smile on her face while Caroline went and then, as if on cue, her father Caroll excused himself.

As soon as they were alone at the table, the icy blast that Terry expected from Sarah came. And there was little she could do but to take it.

"How could you?" Sarah spat the words out angrily. She slammed her fist down on the table so hard that the cups rattled. A splash of coffee fell on a proof sheet. Nearby diners turned to stare.

"What? I—"

"You violated my trust," Sarah hissed.

She knows! Terry thought in a panic. *But how could she? Would Brad stoop so low as to tell her?*

"Why didn't you tell me you knew Brad when you were in school?" Sarah demanded.

"Knew Brad?" Terry repeated with great relief as the truth began to dawn on her. "Is *that* why you're so upset, Sarah?"

"That is most certainly why I'm upset," Sarah huffed. "I'm not used to being lied to by people whom I hire."

"I never lied to you," Terry stated with indignant conviction.

"Well, you didn't tell the full truth," Sarah insisted, sounding as if she could be persuaded to back down from her pinnacle of outrage.

"I told you everything that was pertinent. The fact that I went to college with Bradford Andrews was *not* pertinent to my abilities as a professional photographer. Besides," she added, knowing the question was risky, "would you have *considered* hiring me if you had known?"

Lighting another cigarette, Sarah thought for a moment. "I suppose not," she admitted. "I suppose

I was too much the concerned mother that day." Idly, she picked up one of the proof sheets and began to study it for the first time. While examining it, she said, "I suppose if I were in your place I would have been reticent also."

"Thank you," Terry said quickly, genuinely grateful for Sarah's admission. "I appreciate that."

"No, it's nothing," Sarah muttered, dismissing Terry's comment with a wave of her hand. "Let's just forget this little conversation, shall we?" She picked up another proof sheet.

"Of course," Terry agreed. She was unable to resist asking, "But how did you know—that Brad and I were in school together?"

Sarah continued to peruse the proof sheets, "Oh, I just happened to look through that little biography that they handed out in the gallery; it had your dates for college. And I happened to know that Brad was there at the same time. But I believe that he would have been several years ahead of you, so you couldn't have known each other *very* well. . . ."

Terry decided on the spot that she wouldn't skirt the truth; if the question came, she would answer it. She waited for the raised eyebrow, the piercing glance, the look that would signal that the big question was coming—"Just how well did you know Brad in college" or "Have you kept the promise you made to me?"—but Sarah continued to study the proof sheets in silence. Much to Terry's surprise and relief, she said nothing, except . . .

"These are really quite good, my dear."

"Why . . . thank you. I—I . . ."

"Yes, dear?" Sarah looked up at her with a questioning expression. "Is there something the matter?"

"I'm just a little surprised. I thought I was about to be dismissed."

"Oh no, not on your life," Sarah said expansively. "These first pictures fully justify our faith in you, dear. No, by all means, continue. We want you and Brad to get right out there and finish up as quickly as you can, starting first thing tomorrow. . . ."

"Tomorrow?"

"Oh, didn't I tell you? How absentminded of me. Brad should be back in town by tonight, and I know he's just all eager to get going again, to finish up this part of our project. I do hope tomorrow's convenient for you. There's only so much time that dear Brad can give us, and he's been most generous so far."

Terry was in shock, but Caroll and Caroline's return just then covered her confusion.

"Well then, dear," Sarah asked again, just as soon as her husband and daughter had settled back in, "do we have an understanding? Are you all ready to go again in the morning?"

Terry felt boxed in, but by whom and for what purpose she couldn't begin to say. She agreed meekly to Sarah's request. "Tomorrow morning is fine," she said in a little soft voice. To herself she was beginning to sound as childish as Brad's fiancée.

"Good, I'll pass the word along," Sarah declared in a brisk, businesslike fashion.

"Fine," Terry agreed again. She knew she had to seize this opportunity to leave before her tenuous composure unraveled completely. It didn't help her to notice that the phone call had done wonders for Caroline's mood and that her depression was gone, the woeful expression replaced by a bright, bubbly smile.

"I really should be going. I have lots to do to be

ready by the morning." She gathered up her magnifying glass and dug out a small manila envelope from the bottom of her bag. "These are some prints of the best shots and some of the negatives. It was all I had time to do." She handed the envelope to Caroll, who took it gratefully.

"This is most efficient of you, Miss Rovik," he observed. "Very commendable, and much faster than we expected."

"Thank you." Terry said her goodbyes quickly and left.

Outside on the busy plaza, she paused a moment to catch her breath and to let her eyes adjust to the bright, midday Chicago sun. She rummaged in her bag for her sunglasses, ignoring the appreciative wolf-whistles of two passing construction workers; after the tension of the lunch with the entire McMasters family, a little good-natured leering certainly wasn't going to faze her.

She knew she should consider herself lucky to have gotten out of the restaurant with her big-break job and her reputation both intact. So why, she wondered, didn't she feel lucky? She also knew that she now faced at least two more days in the wilds with Brad, and *that* prospect she should find *un*lucky, not to mention *un*pleasant and downright disgusting. *So why,* she wondered, *didn't she? Moreover, what on earth was she doing feeling butterflies of thrilling anticipation?*

Terry Rovik, you're a fool! she muttered as she crossed the plaza and went toward the parking garage. On the long drive back home, she had plenty of time to dwell on her problems.

Why would Brad bother to continue their book project? The answer, although simple, was not very flattering. He was doing it for his future in-laws and his wife-to-be, of course, bringing their prestigious, but small, publishing company the gift of his immense popularity. And she, Terry realized, was no more than one of Brad's little perks, a bit of decoration for his vacation, perhaps even his final fling. And what a bonus that she was an excellent photographer.

So why was she continuing with this damned project, she asked herself. Where was her pride? This answer, too, was simple: she *was* an excellent photographer, and this was her big chance! That she hadn't kept strictly to business and had allowed Brad to turn her head was her own fault. Her only excuse was that she cared for him—*yes,* to be brutally honest with herself, *loved him*—even more than she cared for herself. But that was a mistake she would not allow herself to make again. She *had* to put herself first. *Had* to!

There were only a few more stops left on their journey—Indiana, Iowa, western Nebraska. She would do her job and keep her distance, she told herself. Any hopes that Brad might entertain for an encore of that lakeside performance in some sylvan glade they'd encounter would be instantly quashed. She would make certain of it! And then, in a few days, it would all be over and she would never see Bradford Andrews again as long as she lived.

By the time Terry turned into her quiet residential street, with its rows of graceful shade trees, the nearby junior high school had already let out for the day. She passed knots of giggling school kids, boys and girls on bicycles weaving down the street in single file, and the usual parade of traveling frisbee players. She pulled into her driveway with only a brief glance at the wine-red Jaguar XJ6 that was parked across the street from her house and surrounded by a crowd of gawking teenagers. She got right out of the old Chevy and started toward the front porch.

"Terry, wait," the familiar voice called out to her. The crowd of admiring youngsters parted to make way for the handsome man, wearing a navy blazer and gray slacks, who hopped out of the Jag.

Terry looked over her shoulder but kept walking, so that Brad wasn't able to catch up with her until she was almost at the front door. His strong hand grasping her at the elbow stopped her determined forward motion and spun her around.

"Hey there, it's me." With one hand on each of her shoulders, he held her at arm's length, like someone drinking in the sight of a long-lost friend.

Afraid that he might try to hug her, or worse, Terry shook free of his grip. "I know it's you," she said tersely, stepping back.

Brad gave her one of his famous boyish grins and asked, "Well then, just what's going on here?"

"Why are you waiting outside my house?" Terry countered.

Brad looked sheepish. "Because your friend Millie wouldn't let me *inside*, that's why."

"Good for her."

"Hey!" Brad sounded hurt. "Do you think she still holds my rudeness at the airport against me? I tried to apologize, but she wouldn't give me half a chance. . . ."

"Maybe she doesn't like to hear how her friend got dumped off in some little Michigan town by the Hotshot Journalist. Did you ever think of that?"

"Oh. Look here, Terry, I tried to apologize to you that night, I tried to explain . . ."

"Explain! Explain *what?* You explained nothing, you just waltzed down the stairs and said, 'Sorry. Duty calls. Bye'—and left." Looking past Brad's shoulder, Terry noticed that the crowd of kids, most of them girls with notebooks and pens at the ready for autographs, had edged onto her lawn, and that those in the front were giggling and whispering and making no secret of trying to overhear.

Terry lowered her voice to an angry whisper. "Just wham, bam and not even a 'thank you ma'am.' Is that your idea of an explanation? Not word *one* to show that you even remembered we were in the very same 'romantic little place' where I once waited for you to return after you proposed to me. . . ."

"But, Terry—"

"And instead of Prince Charming I get a distinctly *un*charming telegram, saying, 'Sorry, kid, but I've decided to seek my fortune as a foreign correspondent.' You think you can do that to me *twice* in the same place. Just who do you take me for, anyway?"

"But, Terry, I'm trying to apologize, I'm trying to explain. . . ."

"Well?" Terry folded her hands across her chest. "I'm listening."

"I *am* sorry, deeply sorry. About that first time,

well, I've kicked myself and called myself a fool more times than you ever could. All I can say is that if I hadn't gone, if I hadn't grabbed that one opportunity, it would have been a different kind of agony—an agony of not knowing, an agony of always wondering—and eventually it would have come between us. I think you can see that, too. . . ."

"Go on," Terry said, in no mood to concede anything. "What about *this* time?"

Brad looked down at the ground and sighed. "I asked you to trust me," he mumbled.

"What? 'Trust' you? Are you kidding? You mean you're starting *that* mumbo-jumbo *again?* I don't believe it."

Brad looked up, his eyes blazing. "Listen to me, *please:* all I ask is that you trust me for one more day. Just one single day. I couldn't tell you then why I had to rush back to New York, and I can't tell you now. Believe me, I wish I could. But I promise, by tomorrow night I'll be able to tell you *everything*. One way or another," Brad added, sounding definitely cryptic and possibly fatalistic, "I'll tell you everything then. Okay?"

"All right," Terry agreed curtly.

Brad's face lit up. "Really? You'll trust me until tomorrow night? You'll wait twenty-four hours for my explanation? That's terrific, Terry." He reached out to touch her shoulder, but she sidestepped his touch.

"Trust has nothing to do with it, *Mr*. Andrews," she observed coldly. *"I'm* a professional photographer with an assignment to finish. Unfortunately, for me to be able to do that, *your* presence is required. *There-*

fore, tomorrow I'll be there to listen to your precious explanation. I expect I'll get a good laugh out of it. But *that* is all I expect."

Brad grimaced, looking for all the world as if she'd slapped him. "But you are coming? You'll be ready early in the morning for me to pick you up for the drive down?"

"That's right. I'll be ready. The sooner we start, the sooner we finish, and the better I like it."

"So you don't trust me." Brad frowned. "You really don't care *what* my explanation is. You're just out for a little fame and fortune yourself."

Terry tilted her head back and gave him a full look of pride and anger. "Your right on all counts," she snapped. "I wouldn't trust you as far as I could throw you *and* your fancy red car! The time is long past for *any* of *your* explanations! And you can bet on it that it's my turn!"

With that Terry turned, quickly opened the door, walked inside, and without looking back slammed the door in Brad's face. Immediately she turned the dead-bolt lock.

To her surprise, Millie was standing next to the door. "That's tellin' him," she said in a fierce whisper, adding, "I was right here, I couldn't help over-hearing."

Terry leaned against the door, feeling suddenly exhausted by her outburst, and brushed her straight blond hair out of her eyes. "That's okay, Millie," she said distractedly.

Millie stepped over to one of the front windows and peeked out. "Look, he's leaving," she whispered.

Outside, Brad pushed his way through the crowd

of excited, autograph-seeking teens, got back into the red Jaguar, and roared off, leaving the disappointed kids to mill around behind him. It was the first time, Terry noted with astonishment, that she had ever seen him fail to sign an autograph or be less than polite to one of his fans.

chapter 8

LIKE EVERY OTHER great city, Chicago in the pearly light of dawn had the quality of an ancient artifact—monumental, timeless, and somewhat eerie. Terry was fascinated by the way it looked, and as she and Brad drove out of town in the Jaguar, she got out a camera, rolled down her window and shot frame after frame, hoping to capture the quiet city's angularities, textures, and shadings for her personal collection. Beside her Brad drove with the same single-minded concentration with which he piloted his silver airplane.

They raced south on Interstate 65. It was a humid, summery morning, more like late July than late May, but inside the smoothly humming automobile the atmosphere was distinctly frigid.

"The Wabash," Brad noted as they passed over the famous river.

Click, click. Terry snapped two frames out the window of the speeding Jag.

"We're making good time," he observed, "maybe we'll be able to turn west later and get in a stop at the river. Somewhere down by Vincennes, on the Indiana-Illinois line would be nice."

"Sure," Terry replied tonelessly, "if there's time."

Brad began to hum "When It's Moonlight on the Wabash" in his familiar off-key manner. Carrying a tune, Terry remembered, was *not* one of his talents.

"What about the radio?" she suggested.

"Great idea."

They reached for the radio at the same instant and their fingers touched. Terry recoiled.

Brad turned the knob and a big-band jazz number with a nice traveling beat came blaring out of the car's stereo speakers. He tapped his fingers on the steering wheel in time to the music, while she sat in strained silence, her hands in her lap, and wished her fingers that had just brushed his hand didn't feel as if they'd been burned. It was ridiculous, she knew, although it was a good five minutes before the sensation faded.

Onward they went, not exchanging a single word for the next half hour. Brad kept busy navigating the Jaguar around the outskirts of metropolitan Indianapolis, while Terry let her eyes drift over the wide, flat Midwestern horizon.

A few minutes later, he said, "We're crossing 40," as they went over a nondescript divided highway.

"So?"

"Very historic. This used to be called the Cumberland Road, the first national highway. The pioneers took it to go west to St. Louis."

"Oh? Is this another one of your fascinating research-department tidbits?"

"I'm just trying to make conversation. . . ."

More time went by. The sleek red Jaguar carried them into the hilly wooded country of the southern part of the state. They left the main highways in favor of lightly traveled two-lane country roads. All around them, wildflowers were in bloom.

Despite the heat, Brad turned off the air conditioner and lowered the windows. The scent of flowering lilac was in the air.

"We're making excellent time now," he said. "It shouldn't be long. Great little car, this Jag," he added, patting the steering wheel.

Terry took out her camera, stopped down the shutter speed and took another picture out the window as they passed a patch of dainty flowering bluets. With the lowered shutter speed bringing out the motion of the car racing by, she hoped to get a photograph that was nearly abstract, with just a few petals standing out in the midst of a swirl of blue and white and green.

The bluets, Terry remembered, were also known as Quaker Ladies and Innocence flowers. She decided then that sitting in silence any longer would be petulant; after all, they still had to work together and the talk couldn't be more neutral. She cleared her throat.

"I didn't know you had a Jaguar," she said.

"Oh I don't," Brad answered enthusiastically. "It's rented."

"Rented?" She couldn't keep the sarcasm out of her voice. "I didn't know you could rent a car like this."

He ignored her tone. "Sure, you can rent anything

if you've got the money. You see, I'm thinking of buying one of these, so I figured it would be a good idea to take one out for a spin."

"'Take one out for a spin?'" Terry repeated in a disbelieving voice. "Just who are you trying to impress?"

Brad ignored her challenging question. "We could've flown in the Beechcraft, but I decided to leave it back at O'Hare for a thorough maintenance check. You can't be too careful with a plane, you know. It's a good little aircraft, but I've been pushing it hard lately and I wouldn't want anything to go wrong."

He arched his back and yawned. Keeping his hands on the steering wheel, he rolled his shoulders forward, then back. When he glanced over at Terry there was a gleam in his eye. "I'm glad we're almost there. My back is getting kind of stiff. You wouldn't want to—"

"Not a chance!" she said emphatically. She crossed her legs and folded her arms across her chest and sat that way until they pulled into the entrance of the Muscatatuck Wildlife Park a few minutes later.

Brad wheeled the Jaguar in among the campers and jeeps in the parking lot. It took only a few minutes for them to check in and get directions to the wooded forest trails that crisscrossed the seven-thousand-acre refuge. Once again, they were expected and, much to Terry's irritation, Brad was greeted like a king come to mingle with his subjects.

They were dressed for another day in the woods. He had on baggy walking shorts and a collarless white shirt. She was wearing jeans and a denim jacket over a silk, spaghetti-strap white camisole. While she waited for Brad to sign autographs and pick up maps of the refuge, she took off the jacket and stuffed it into her pack. It wasn't long before they were just two lone hikers, with light packs on their backs, marching down a trail that followed the meandering Muscatatuck River.

Unlike the first part of their expedition, this last leg was to places Terry had never been—places to which Brad had come as a child with his family—so she was able to take in the diverse and lush scenery with a new, detached appreciation for its many beauties, and to listen with a renewed interest as Brad dictated into his cassette recorder while they walked along the wooded trail.

"My parents brought me here many times when I was a child," Brad said into the machine, while Terry, walking beside him, snapped away at a white-tailed deer across the trail in front of them. "We would drive down from Chicago to Indianapolis for the weekend," he continued, "to stay with my father's brother, a well-known local journalist. While my mother organized nature tours and went bird-watching, my father and his brother, both avid hunters, would take me to the Muscatatuck for a day of duck hunting."

Brad turned off the cassette recorder. "Of course, that was before they made this a wildlife refuge, and the ducks weren't protected then," he added to Terry, who was a longtime opponent of hunting in any form except with a camera.

"Sure," she said, sighting through her viewfinder on a cardinal and a bluebird that had both just come to rest on nearby branches of the same tree. "You don't have to explain to me."

Brad switched on the recorder again. "The Algonquin Indians named this area Muscatatuck," he noted, "or 'Land of Winding Waters.' I've always thought that it more than lives up to its name. In fact, you could say that it was right here, during many a long lazy day of following the winding waters with my parents and my uncle, that I developed both my abiding love of nature and my lifelong interest in journalism. . . ."

Brad stopped, switched off the recorder again and looked around. "You know, it kind of looks familiar around here," he said, a tinge of rising excitement in his voice. He crossed the narrow trail, walking over to the top of a leafy, tree-covered embankment that descended steeply all the way to the river below. "I sort of remember that bend and that big black rock sticking out like a finger and that oak growing there, only it was much smaller then. . . ."

He pushed his way past the overhanging branches of the birch and ash trees that grew up from the side of the embankment. Slipping and sliding and grabbing on to branches to keep from falling, he made his way down the steep slope. He hurried over to the edge of the river, right to the side of a pin oak growing there.

"This is just great!" he called out, pointing excitedly up at the tree. "Look, Terry, my initials—B.A.—and the date. This is where I carved my initials when I was ten years old! It was the very day my father gave me my first pocket knife. . . ."

"Hey, Brad."

"What?" He turned—a big smile on his face, his finger still pointing at the tree—and looked up at her.

"Say 'cheese.' " Terry clicked off two shots before he had a chance to move a muscle. "We can put that one on the book's back cover," she said with a smile, "and call it 'Portrait of the Author as an Excited Little Boy.' "

Brad put his hands on his hips and gave her one of his famous self-deprecating grins. "C'mon, get a close-up."

"Down *there?*"

"Sure, just be careful, work your way down slowly. It's easy."

Terry shrugged off her pack and began to make her way gingerly down the steep embankment. She came down leaning far back, her heels digging into the soft earth, letting herself practically fall from tree to tree, until she reached the last small rise above the placid river's bank. Brad was standing just below her.

"Almost there," he said, stretching out a muscular arm. "I'll give you a hand."

"No, thank you, I'm quite capable of making it the rest of the way myself."

As Terry said this, she was standing, arms held gracefully out from her sides for extra balance, on the edge of a little knoll about four feet above the riverbank. She took one tiny, careful step forward and the rich bottomland soil crumbled beneath her.

With a little cry of surprise she fell right into Brad's waiting arms. "Oh!"

Holding her tightly, he grinned down at her. "I wish I had a camera," he observed dryly. He leaned down and kissed her lightly, affectionately, on the cheek.

Immediately, Terry struggled free of his embrace.

"What's that for?" she asked, brushing herself off.

Brad shrugged. "That's just 'cause you're so cute."

Terry refused to acknowledge how endearing he and that remark were. Instead, she frowned up at him and said, "I thought we had an understanding. No more funny business!"

"Have it your way," he said serenely, stepping back beside the old oak. "If you snap your picture, we can get a move on. Does that suit you, *Madam* Photographer?"

"You bet it does," she retorted, irritated by his continuing calm. As she focused through the viewfinder on him, standing next to the tree with his initials carved in its trunk, she couldn't help but see that his look continued to be unruffled and unworried. It wasn't the oily look of the seducer or the guilty look of the philanderer. He didn't look nervous, he didn't look ashamed, he didn't look intimidated by her righteous anger. Terry had to admit to herself that he hadn't looked bothered all day.

She remembered what he had said about trusting him for one more day, how everything would be explained. *What exactly did he have in mind?* She knew Brad Andrews well enough to realize there was no point in asking—he would tell her in his own good time. She also knew that the only thing *she* could do was to keep her guard up while attending to the business at hand.

So she snapped several more shots of him and his beloved oak tree, then took nearly an entire roll of film of the beautiful wood ducks that graced this part of the quiet river.

"Too bad most of the males already are down to

their summer feathers," Brad observed, picking up from the water's edge a bright blue feather, tipped with scarlet and gold, and holding it out for Terry's inspection.

"Hold it up to the light," she said, focusing her camera on the feather and snapping several more shots. "That's okay," she added, "the ducks still looked pretty spectacular and I got a few nice angles when that big flock of them took off from the water together."

Soon, she and Brad made their way back up from the riverbank to the winding trail. They walked back to the parking lot at the visitors' center in silence. By the time they were in the Jag and once again out on the road heading west, it was still only midafternoon.

But it was nearly dinner time when they finally crossed the Indiana-Illinois border, a line that was defined by the broad, silt-filled Wabash River.

Once in Illinois, Brad pulled the Jag in at a rest stop near the wooded state park that was their destination and hopped out to make a phone call. Terry got out of the car and did stretching exercises on the grassy lawn, until the appreciative whistles and lecherous looks of a nearby carload of rowdy college students forced her to stop.

When Brad returned several minutes later, he was muttering something about "Board meetings in New York that never seemed to end," but Terry's tentative attempts to get him to explain were fruitless.

Instead, he asked if she minded waiting a couple of hours more before eating.

"Not at all. It's a little too hot and muggy to be

hungry anyway. What have you got in mind?"

"Let's make a quick tour of the park while we still have the light. It's definitely worth the stop.

"There's a nice place down near Mt. Carmel, where I used to stop with my folks, a kind of country inn where we can get rooms for the night and have some dinner. Okay with you?"

Terry couldn't resist asking, in a teasing voice, "And do I get your long-awaited explanation for dessert?"

Brad frowned. "At dinner," he answered soberly, "we'll talk about tomorrow's schedule, our future plans. And I'll explain everything—*no matter what.* The hell with whether or not they're ready back on the East Coast! I've waited long enough. . . ."

Terry found the state park to be an enchanting place; with its massive specimens of a wide variety of trees, it was a nature photographer's dream, and she clicked happily away at the giant oaks, walnuts, and silver maples all around her.

But Brad remained preoccupied and seemed nervous. It was obvious that the phone call had upset him; Terry could tell from the terse, clipped way he talked into his cassette recorder and how he paced the bank of the Wabash while he recorded his notes, oblivious both to the river and the splendid tall trees.

"The two hundred acres of forest that comprise Beall State Park are one of the few remaining examples of pristine bottomland 'swamp forest' left standing," he said into the recorder.

"A swamp forest," he explained, "grows in a river valley which is subject to periodic flooding. When the river overflows its banks, it deposits rich silt and creates the fertile soil so hospitable to the growth of these massive trees.

"Once, swamp forests grew all along the banks of the major rivers in the Midwest. Not only the Wabash, but the Mississippi and Illinois Rivers, too, were then the sites of thousands of acres of dense forest. But, except for a few places such as this park, the forests are all gone now. Flood control and irrigation projects, land reclamation, farming and lumbering interests..."

With a sigh Brad switched off the cassette recorder. "How depressing," he grumbled.

"I'd say that a white oak that's a good hundred and twenty feet tall is pretty uplifting, actually," she said, pointing up at the magnificent tree whose crown, catching the light of the setting sun, looked like it was on fire. "As long as there are even a few places like this left, things can't be *that* bad."

"You should've seen it before, when I came here as a kid," he protested, refusing to be cheered up. "What do you say we get going? I don't think I'm really in the mood for the glories of nature just now. Okay?"

Terry shrugged. "I'm losing the light anyway. Just one more shot first." She indicated the spot near the riverbank where she'd set up a camera on a tripod. "I'm using a new filter," she said, taking the shot, then beginning to dismantle her equipment. "See that tiny strip of light right on the horizon," she added, pointing to the west, "it's kind of a light lime color. I'm trying to bring it out from the background."

"Yeah, I've seen that light before," Brad said, as they walked back through the fading light of dusk to the red Jaguar. "That's what my Grandpa called 'tornado-weather light.' He used to say, 'When the temperature and the humidity get up above ninety, and the sky looks like it's full of sea water, then watch out for the big storm coming.' Of course, it's still a little early in the season to be worrying about anything like that."

The Jag was cruising smoothly down the two-lane highway, its headlamps cutting through the lonely rural night. Brad was looking out for the country inn he remembered fondly from his youth, but the stately, white, neoclassical villa he described was nowhere to be found.

"I suppose it could be anywhere in southeast Illinois," he muttered, gripping the steering wheel tightly.

Terry smiled indulgently. "I sure don't see it." For her, the day that had started out so unpleasantly was ending on a relaxing note. The outdoor work, scenery, and exercise had helped, and so had the new insights into Brad's background. She found his excitement at finding his initials and his concern about the vanishing forestlands quite touching. Even his inability to find the country inn or to resolve whatever it was that was so bothering him and keeping him from making his grand explanation melted Terry's resolve to keep an icy formality between them.

"Look, Brad—" Terry nodded toward a distant glow ahead of them. "Maybe that's it. Why don't we stop there, at least, and ask directions."

"Okay." Brad stepped on the accelerator and the Jaguar responded with a new surge of power.

Terry looked at him. He was hunched over the wheel, his handsome features set in an expression of single-pointed intensity. "How's your back?" she asked softly. "Still stiff?"

"It's okay," he muttered.

Terry shook her head. "If you don't want to talk . . ."

Brad glanced at her before turning his eyes back to the road. "Sorry, I'm preoccupied is all . . . and I wish I could find that inn. I know it used to be somewhere right along here. . . ."

"You know, Brad, I have to admit I was pretty skeptical about this book project of ours," Terry said reflectively. "I couldn't understand why you were doing it. I mean, I know you're a native of the Midwest, just like I am. . . ."

"It's the main qualification for my job," he interjected with a sarcastic little chuckle, adding, "no accent, you see."

Terry laughed too. "That's what I couldn't understand: why would you want to come back to the Midwest, bring attention to your background? But I finally figured it out today. . . ."

"*Oh,* did you?"

"I think so," Terry replied, ignoring his taunting tone. "You still love this country, don't you? You've got a real feeling for the heartland. Am I right?"

Brad seemed to think this over. "Yes, you could say that. Yes, you're *partly* right. In fact, that's probably the very reason I got involved in doing a book in the first place."

"What do you mean?" Terry asked curiously, as they drew nearer to the glowing lights, near enough to tell they came from a tall, hotel-like building off to the side of the highway.

"Well, I was at a dinner party in New York a few

months back—black-tie, elegant, ambassadors and the like from all over the world—and there I was holding forth about how this part of the country was not only the heartland but the backbone of the nation as well. I went on and on—to the French ambassador and his wife, I believe—about how, like many others, I had to see the world and travel for many years before I could begin to appreciate the beauties of my native region. I pointed out to them just how beautiful parts of this land are. They sat there, sipping their cognacs and smoking their expensive cigars, listening to me go on about how parts of Minnesota reminded me of the Dutch lake country, how Iowa looked like the plains of central Europe, and how reminiscent the north shore of Lake Superior is of parts of the coast of Bretagne.

"Of course, Caroline McMasters was there," Brad continued, oblivious to how Terry stiffened at the mention of her name, "and she introduced me to her parents, who were also there that night. And one of them—I think it was her father—said to me, 'You should do a book about that part of the country some day.' And I said, 'Some day I will, and perhaps you'll publish it.' He said they'd be delighted. A few months later the opportunity came, and I went to them and said, 'Remember our dinner-party talk? Well, here's the chance to do it.' They were eager to begin, especially when I told them what a limited schedule I was on and how the whole thing had to be finished during my vacation. So here I am," he concluded, wheeling the Jag into the driveway in front of the ten-story hotel, planted in the deserted countryside, whose well-lighted front entrance and large glowing neon sign they had seen from a distance.

"I'll be right back," he said. He parked the car and ran up the hotel's front steps. Terry could see him through the glass double doors in the red-carpeted lobby, talking to the desk clerk behind a wood-paneled front desk.

Reminiscing had lightened Brad's mood, but the mention of his fiancée had darkened Terry's. While waiting in the Jaguar, she once again resolved to follow her original plan and not to be taken in by Brad's boyish charms. It was hard for her to believe that she had let herself get involved with Brad again. If it wasn't for his book, and the chance to include her photographs, she would never have dared to risk getting close to him. *One more day, maybe two,* she reminded herself, *then it's all finished and Brad goes back to Caroline McMasters; that's one fact he can never explain away.*

There was a smile on his face when he came running down the hotel stairs with a bellboy in tow.

"It's all set," he told her happily, "we've got two rooms up on the tenth floor—not that there's anything to see—and they're going to keep the restaurant open for us after hours. How's that for service?" he asked, opening the door for her.

Terry declined to take the hand he held out. "Just the usual star treatment, right?" she noted acidly, stepping out of the Jag. "Anyway, what happened to your famous old country inn? Don't tell me you gave up on it."

Brad gave her a sly grin. "Actually, it was the other way around," he observed.

"What?"

He pointed wordlessly to the sign above the hotel's all-glass front entrance. "Progress," he intoned.

The sign read, *"Welcome, Traveler, to the New Country Inn."*

Terry had showered and changed to a simple red and purple paisley dinner dress but she still couldn't shake the black mood that had descended on her at the mention of Brad's fiancée.

Looking into the bathroom mirror, she held a matching silk scarf against the spun gold of her blond hair and decided against using the scarf as a headband. Sighing as she looked at her face in the mirror, Terry knew it was hopeless: she was just a plainly attractive all-American girl from Chicago, maybe just a little too bright for her own good; how could *she* ever hope to compete with a tall blond goddess type like Caroline McMasters, who was a publishing heiress and a world traveler to boot?

While she combed out her hair and slipped a shawl over her shoulders, unexpected tears welled up in Terry's eyes, but she blinked them back. The scandalous thoughts she found herself thinking certainly didn't help—thoughts like, *it's probably our last night together ever, so why not?*—nor did the fantasies that crossed her mind as she took one more look at herself in the mirror, fantasies in which she boldly threw herself at Brad, heedless of the consequences. . . .

She pushed those silly notions, and the torrid memories that prompted them, out of her mind and went downstairs. But instead of going directly to the restaurant where she and Brad had agreed to meet, Terry stepped into the dark, smoky little piano bar next door to it and ordered a drink.

There were a few tourist couples at little tables around the piano, listening as the middle-aged man in the tuxedo played a medley of standards. At the other end of the small bar from where Terry sat on a red Naugahyde stool was a huge mountain of a man, dressed in a checked sports shirt, a seersucker jacket, and matching slacks. He had a big, round, sunburned face topped by a fuzzy crewcut, and a prominent pot-belly. He was well over six feet tall and must have weighed at least two hundred and fifty pounds.

The red-vested bartender, who had been putting the latest of several bottles of beer in front of the big man, immediately came over to Terry.

He wiped off the bar counter in front of her, put a coaster down and smiled in a friendly, avuncular way. "What can I do for you, ma'am?"

"A Manhattan, please."

"Comin' right up."

After a few seconds of mixing her drink at the other end of the bar, the bartender was back. He placed the frothy drink on the coaster. "One Manhattan cocktail," he said with a craftsman's pride.

Terry reached for her little black purse. "How much will that be?"

The bartender dried off a shot glass. "Nothin', ma'am. Compliments of Big Jerry." He nodded in the direction of the crewcut man in the seersucker jacket, who smiled shyly.

Terry whispered to the bartender. "Oh, I couldn't. Tell him thank you, but I just couldn't."

Still drying the glass, the bartender whispered

back, "Actually, ma'am, I would if I was you. Y'see, Big Jerry's harmless, but he *is* awfully big and he's been drinkin' quite a while now. He says you remind him of his wife Lillie, back home in Tennessee. He's a trucker, ma'am, and he stops here often. I seen him get like this when he gets all misty for his Lillie. He blubbers into his beer awhile, then goes to bed. Ain't nothin' to it. Underneath he's just a big teddy bear is all."

Terry was dubious. "You *sure?*"

"Yes, ma'am," the bartender replied.

"Then please tell Big Jerry thank you, and tell him I hope he's reunited with his Lillie very soon."

"Yes, ma'am."

The bartender walked back to Big Jerry and conveyed Terry's message in a loud whisper that carried back to her. When he got to the part about being reunited really soon, Terry could hear Big Jerry's snuffling. She realized that the piano was starting on "The Tennessee Waltz" for the second time.

The bartender came back. "Big Jerry's respects, ma'am. He wonders if you'd join him for a few moments."

"Did he request 'The Tennessee Waltz'?" Terry asked quizzically.

"Yes, ma'am, he gave the piano player a twenty-dollar bill and told him to play the song until the money ran out or the bar closed. Old Jerry's really upset tonight."

"He's harmless, you say?"

"Yes, ma'am."

"You're sure?"

"Positively. He's from the old school, ma'am, and

wouldn't dream of hurtin' women or children or dogs."

"Well . . . tell him *he* may join *me,* but just for one drink. Then I have to leave."

"Yes, *ma'am.*"

Soon Big Jerry was ambling over, approaching shyly, a hang-dog expression on his beet red face, like some big friendly mutt hoping for a pat on the head.

"Thank you, little lady." He settled his massive bulk onto the stool next to her. "I appreciate this. I been on the road two days straight and I had no one to talk to and nothin' to think 'bout 'cept my Lillie." Big Jerry's voice quavered. "Truly, little lady, in that nice dress you do remind me of her; you're both just as pretty as could be."

To Terry, Big Jerry's sincerity was obvious. "Call me Terry," she said. "Are you on your way home to Lillie now?"

"No . . . Terry, that's just it, I'm not even half done with my run. I got to go up to Chicago yet, then all the way up to Detroit, before I start back. I tell you, long-haul truckin's no way for a happily married man to live," Big Jerry said emphatically, taking a big gulp of beer.

"You know, little lady, I been stoppin' here regular almost three years. Tonight, I got in just a little later than usual. You think they'd make me up a couple hamburgers and a cold beer, give me a little table in the corner. *No way!*

"So I come down to the bar so's I can get that beer at least, and you know what? The damn restaurant is open again!

"'Hey, what's goin' on here?' I ask, when the damn waiter stops me at the door again and says I can't go in because it's a private party.

"And that waiter has the nerve to tell me that this damn bigshot TV guy, this Bradley Andrew fellah, is here and they opened up special just for him! How do you like that nerve?"

"I don't," Terry said immediately, "not at all. But I've got to tell you, I'm *with* this bigshot TV guy. . . ."

"Oh." Big Jerry looked morose. He hung his head. "I'm sorry if I offended you, little lady," he mumbled, "but I just don't think that kind of treatment is right."

"No offense taken," Terry replied. "In fact, I agree with you completely. I've been having my own problems along those very lines actually. . . ."

Big Jerry's head shot up, an angry look on his face. "This bigshot TV guy ain't been treatin' you right? If you've been gettin' bad treatment, you just say the word. . . ."

Just then, all conversation in the bar stopped, the piano player missed a beat, and even the bartender just stood there with his mouth open: Bradford Andrews himself was framed in the open doorway!

The way Brad entered the darkened bar, with one hand in the pocket of his gray silk sports jacket and the other hanging loosely at his side, with his hair brushed neatly to one side and his tanned, handsome face flashing his most telegenic, charismatic smile, reminded Terry of Prince Charles or one of the Kennedys. The sight of him melted her heart, although right then she would rather have undergone any torture than to tell him so.

Still smiling warmly, Brad walked over to her. But

as soon as he saw that she was at the bar with another man, the smile vanished.

"Ah, there you are," he said lightly, stepping into the space between her and Big Jerry. "I've been looking all over for you."

"Brad, I want you to meet someone. . . ."

He didn't even glance over his shoulder. "Excuse us," he said, taking Terry by the arm. "I've got terrific news. . . ."

Terry pulled free of his grip. *"Brad!* Just one minute, I'm not ready to leave yet. . . ."

Again Brad reached out for her and again Terry evaded his touch. Heedlessly, he leaned over and whispered in her ear, "Let's go to the restaurant where we can be alone. I've got something important to say to you."

Brad's eyes were dancing, Terry noticed, and a broad smile was quivering at the corner of his lips, but she was having none of it. "Bradford Andrews, you're being rude to this gentleman, and we've already put him out once. I'm sure it wasn't intentional, but . . ."

Brad grinned at her, looking like a happy kid unable to hold a secret a second longer: he hadn't heard a word she'd been saying. "Terry, please, let's go. I'll even come back and sign autographs later, if you want. Okay?"

He leaned closer and tried to kiss her cheek, but Terry pulled her face back. "Bradford Andrews, you're being insufferable!" She stood up. "I'm leaving."

"What?" Brad grabbed her by the arm. "Where? You can't go anywhere. . . ."

"Oh yes I can."

Without warning, Big Jerry was up, a massive paw on Brad's shoulder. "Just a second, buddy," he growled.

Brad flicked the hand off his shoulder. "Mind your own business, fellow," he said, still looking at Terry, still holding her by the arm.

But Big Jerry was not so easily put off. "I think the little lady said she wanted to leave."

Brad released his hold on Terry's arm. Slowly he turned and faced Big Jerry, who was easily a full head taller and a hundred pounds heavier.

"Listen, Mister, I don't know who you are and I don't care, but I'm telling you to mind your own business. I used to live in Japan and I studied karate, so watch it—understand?"

Big Jerry laughed, a jolly belly laugh. "Fellah said that to me once," he reminisced. "That fellah hit me hard as he could, and you know what? *Nothin' happened*. 'Cept one thing. You know what that was?"

"I think I can guess," Brad said.

Quickly, Terry stepped between the two men. "Don't hurt him," she implored Big Jerry.

"No, little lady, I wouldn't dream of it," Big Jerry replied.

"Terry," Brad began slowly, deliberately, sounding like the very voice of reason, "why don't you come with me now? You've had your fun at my expense, so why don't we go to the restaurant. I have something very important to say to you, and if you don't come now you could ruin everything."

"*I* could ruin everything? What about *you?* Doing what you please and stepping all over other people, butting into their lives and upsetting them without even a second thought or bothering to explain. . . ." Terry paused for breath and realized that it wasn't the inadvertent inconvenience to Big Jerry's plans that she was talking about. Suddenly she felt on the verge of tears again.

"But that's just it," Brad implored, "if you'd only let me I *would* explain. That's what I'm trying to tell you."

"Don't bother."

"Huh?" Brad looked dumbstruck.

"I'm tired of waiting around for your explanations."

But . . ."

"You should've explained when you had a chance. Now it's too late."

"Terry, *please.*" Brad started after her, but his way was blocked by Big Jerry, so he couldn't see the tears that were rolling silently down her cheeks.

"Hold it, fellah," Big Jerry said, putting a huge hand on Brad's chest.

From behind Big Jerry, Terry asked in a small voice, "When did you plan to go back to Chicago, Big Jerry?"

Still holding Brad at bay, Big Jerry turned his head and gave her a huge, pleased grin. "Anytime you say, little lady. Sooner I get there, the sooner I get back to my Lillie."

"Will you take a rider?" Terry asked in a quavering voice.

"You bet I will. Little lady, yer the prettiest thing I ever hauled."

"Terry," Brad protested, but it was too late. Her

mind was made up; in fact, she decided, it was something she should have done long ago.

And so it was that ten minutes later Terry was sitting in the cab of the sixteen-wheeler as it rolled north, knifing through the quiet, summery, black Midwestern night, while mournful country music blared from Big Jerry's tape deck.

And so it was that early the next morning the same junior-high-school students, who only two days earlier had seen her arguing on her front porch with a world famous television personality, were now treated to the sight of her hopping down from the cab of a long-haul sixteen-wheel truck.

By the time the amazed teenagers had arrived in their classrooms, Terry was asleep in her own bed.

chapter 9

FOR THE FIRST time since she was an undergraduate at the university, Terry slept past noon. When she awoke, she slipped into her blue silk kimono and padded barefoot downstairs. Millie was nowhere in sight, but there were several messages in her handwriting on the little oak sewing table at the end of the hallway.

Just as I thought! Terry exclaimed to herself, reading the top note on the stack: "8:30 A.M.—Brad Andrews called, offered me his 'sincere apologies' and asked to talk with you. I said you were asleep and it wasn't possible."

A taste of his own medicine! Terry thought with pleasure, picking up the second note: "9:15 A.M.—

Brad Andrews called again. I said you were still asleep."

Serves him right! Terry told herself, reading the third: "9:45 A.M.—Brad called again. I told him you absolutely could not be disturbed."

There were three more notes in the same vein. The last one had been hurriedly scribbled and was barely legible: "11:30—B.A. phoned *again!* Said he has to talk to you and will wait outside until you come out. I have to leave, but don't worry, everything's locked. See you later today. Love, M."

Terry went over to the front door, cracked it open with the chain lock on and peeked out: sure enough, in a metallic blue Porsche parked at her curbside a familiar face in aviator sunglasses was reading a newspaper with a big headline.

Closing and locking the door again, Terry muttered to herself in exasperation, "Just how many cars does that man have at his disposal?"

She went back to the sewing table where the morning mail was stacked and looked through the bills and advertisements addressed to her, then picked up the manila envelope with her name on it and the return address of a Chicago printing company. The words RUSH and DO NOT BEND were stamped on the outside.

Inside was a glossy, double-sized sheet of fine paper with a small, handwritten note clipped to it. On one half of the sheet was a black and white photograph of a smiling Brad; underneath were the words "Famed Journalist-Author" and below them, in smaller type, a paragraph-long biography.

The other half of the sheet featured a full color photograph of a cute round face with huge yellow and black eyes staring out from behind a mask of silvery feathers. Terry well remembered this face and the incidents surrounding the taking of this photograph of the little saw-whet owl peeping out from the tree on the small island in the middle of the St. Croix River. She could practically hear Brad's tale of the Indian legend of the saw-whet and, for just a moment, could practically feel the heat of his passion for her that afternoon, as well as on the following day.

Lust, she reminded herself, *is all it was.*

Above the shiny photograph of the saw-whet, superimposed over a light, sky blue background, was written the title of the book—*their* book—in imposing black roman type: TRAVELS THROUGH THE HEARTLAND. Underneath the photo of the little owl was added a subtitle: *A Personal Reminiscence,* and below that, the bylines: *Words by Bradford Andrews, Pictures by Terry Rovik.*

Tears came to Terry's eyes. She had expected this moment to be a happy one—her first byline on her first book of photographs—but here she was alone, barefoot and practically undressed, with no one to share it, haunted by the man responsible.

She pulled the kimono tighter around herself and brushed away the tears with the back of one fist. She read the note that was clipped to the glossy mock-up of their book cover:

"Caroll, the sweet dear, had our Chicago printer rush out a mechanical of the cover of The Book. We knew you would be interested in seeing some of your handiwork."

Terry didn't have to read the signature—S. McMasters, President—to recognize the note's author. She knew that only Sarah could imply volumes of innuendo without saying a single improper word.

Slowly and deliberately, she crushed the note in her hand and threw it on the floor. "'Some of your handiwork,' indeed!" she muttered irately to herself. Then she ran back upstairs and began rummaging through her desk. It took her a full five minutes to find what she was looking for: the contract she had signed, after just skimming the pages and pages of impenetrable legalese, with McMasters Publishing.

It took another five minutes for her to locate the relevant paragraph at the bottom of the seventeenth page. She read it and read it again, then read it for the third time to make absolutely certain she understood the meaning of the jargon. It was as she had suspected.

Terry smiled triumphantly to herself. *Nowhere* in that paragraph, and *nowhere* in the contract at all, did it say that she was obligated in any way, shape or form to finish her assignment in the company of *anyone* else—*not* Brad, *not* Sarah, *not a single other soul* if it so pleased her! All that was required of her, according to the contract, was that she go to the various places listed and take "Photographs of satisfactory quality for the proposed book."

As she stripped off her kimono and slipped into a pair of pleated gray shorts, a matching gray and white spotted blouse and sandals, a determined look was on Terry's angular face. She combed her hair and pinned it back with coral-shell barrettes, smiling at last at her fixed expression in the mirror.

There were only two more places on the list in the contract, and *she would go by herself!*

She would send Sarah a telegram—"FINISHING ASSIGNMENT BY MYSELF"—and Sarah would know just what she meant and would probably consider it a victory. But Terry didn't care.

There were lots of other things to worry about: she would leave Millie a note, go out to restock her film supply, check in at the gallery where her exhibit had just ended, make travel arrangements. . . .

The list went on and on. She might not be able to leave before nightfall, or even until the next morning, but at least she wouldn't be sitting around, at the mercy of events.

Terry looked out her front window, down at the street below. The Porsche was still there, and she could just glimpse the edge of the same glossy green and black newspaper through the front windshield. That meant that Brad was still there, waiting and reading. *Good,* she thought, *let him wait as long as he wants*.

Terry stuffed a camera into her old leather shoulder bag, ran downstairs, and slipped out the kitchen door. She crossed the back alley, went through a neighbor's yard and, five minutes later, was boarding a bus for downtown.

She stepped out of the sweltering, humid heat. It was a pall over the old city street of refurbished factories and warehouses, nestled in the shadow of the downtown skyscrapers, that was home to a thriving colony of artists and students. As usual, the whitewashed walls and hardwood floors of the little gallery that had exhibited her photographs seemed cool and soothing to the eye.

"Terry!" Damien, a pudgy, pale aesthete in a white linen caftan, greeted her with his usual open-armed exuberance. "Do come in."

Terry returned Damien's peck, which was, as always, in the near vicinity of her cheek. "Hi, Damien, I'm just stopping by for a minute to pick up my pictures," she said, looking around at the bare white walls of the gallery's empty front room. Gone were the photographs that had brought her and Brad back together—if even for a short and futile time!

Damien followed her unhappy gaze. "It's not the same here without your wonderful vistas of the natural world to delight the eye," he observed gallantly, adding with a sigh, "or to bring in the paying customers." Damien gave her an appraising look. "Are you upset?" he asked solicitously.

"No, I'm fine," Terry replied unconvincingly.

"Are you sure?"

"Yes, really. . . . And thank you for asking and for saying such nice things about my pictures," she said, in a soft voice full of graciousness and modesty. "But I really can't stay, so if you'll just tell me where the photos are . . ."

"Boxed and waiting," Damien replied brightly, knowing Terry well enough not to press her any further. "Come on in back. We're closed to the public for the day to set up the new exhibit."

Damien led the way into the small back room. Terry, her hands jammed into the pockets of her shorts, followed after.

In the gallery's second room a unique sight awaited her: television sets in every model, shape and form! Dozens of them were everywhere—on the floor, on pedestals, affixed to brackets on the wall; from ancient black and white consoles that looked like old radios with tiny oval screens, to the latest-model huge wall projections—and they were all on, all tuned to the same channel, all showing the same afternoon talk show with the sound turned off.

"Good lord, Damien, what's all this?"

"This is what's following your fine exhibition," Damien said with a flourish. "'The Video Environment,' August Paella's latest. Have you heard of him?"

"The conceptual artist from Greece?"

"The very one."

"What a reputation the man has!"

Damien winked at Terry. "It's even worse than the papers say. He's out now, picking up another load of television sets for the exhibit. Actually, Terry dear, if you're in a hurry anyway, I should warn you that he was *very* taken with your photographs and especially that portrait of you we had in the lobby.

"The man's a Zorba-the-Greek type. Who knows what he might do if he saw you, as it were, *in the flesh*."

"Thanks for the suggestion, Damien. I'll just get the photographs and leave. I'm not at all interested in having to fend off some man's advances. . . ."

"Confidentially, dear," Damien said, brushing an invisible dust mote from the front of his caftan, "neither am I. But I tell you, this Paella is not the charlatan everyone makes him out to be. In fact, his theories are rather interesting. He has this Warhol-like idea that the video image is transformed in its power and intensity by the great repetition." Damien made a sweeping gesture that took in all the switched-on TV sets. "Hence all this . . .

"Actually, there's something to the idea," Damien continued, but Terry wasn't listening. She gasped, putting her hand to her mouth, and stepped back as if struck. There, on every screen, was Brad's smiling face—rugged, handsome, mesmerizing in extreme close-up.

Damien followed Terry's startled gaze. "Say, that's that good-looking journalist fellow you're doing a book with, isn't it. I wonder why he's doing the talk-show circuit. I'll turn the sound up on one of these sets."

"*No*. I mean, don't bother for me," Terry said quickly to the puzzled Damien.

"Are you sure you're all right?" he asked.

"Yes, yes I am," Terry insisted, beginning to back out of the room. She was horrified to see that, on every one of the dozens of television sets, Brad's almost princely visage was instantly replaced by a still photograph of the entire McMasters family, a photograph that prominently featured the beautiful Caroline McMasters, every inch the regal princess, seated between her parents.

It was almost impossible to avert her eyes, but at last Terry stepped back through the doorway into the bare front room and away from the hateful images flashing all around her. "I'm going," she called out to the startled Damien.

"But your photos . . ."

"Send them to me, Damien," Terry yelled over her shoulder, her sandals clacking on the hardwood floor as she ran from the room.

Soon she found herself back on the sweltering city street. She hailed a passing taxicab, gave her address, and sank back into the seat, feeling completely unnerved and exhausted.

She knew that the cab fare to her house was a ridiculous extravagance for someone of her limited means, but it wasn't the only extravagant traveling expense she had in mind. She was determined to finish her assignment as soon as possible, so that she would never have to see Brad or any of the McMasterses again, even if it cost her every cent that she would earn from the book.

Terry shuddered involuntarily at the memory of all those images of Brad and the McMasterses. Without the sound, what he had been talking about was impossible for anyone but a lip-reader to say. But for Terry two words had stood out as clearly as if Brad had shouted them:

"Yes," he had said, smiling in answer to the unseen talk-show host's question, just before the picture of the McMasters family had flashed on the screen, *"marriage."*

When she got back to the house, Brad and the blue Porsche were gone and Millie was still out, so Terry made all her airline and rent-a-car reservations and packed once again. Then she walked around the corner to the photographic-supply store where she had worked until taking the assignment for the McMasterses.

As was usual on a slow afternoon, the owner, Art, a balding entrepreneur whose real interest was not in photography but in the bottom line, was leaning on his elbow behind the counter, thumbing through an inventory form and watching a small, nine-inch portable TV.

"Honey!" His greeting had more enthusiasm than he had shown the day his horse finished first at Washington Park. Terry was flabbergasted when he actually came around from behind the counter and gave her a big hug and a kiss. "Let me look at you: Art's Photo Supplies' very own big star! So, how goes the book?"

"Actually, I just came in to buy some more film. I'm going back out today to finish it up."

"Fine, fine. And don't even consider the cost—not even the employee's discount—this is from me, on the house," Art said warmly, scooping up twice as many rolls as Terry could possibly use and pushing them into her hands.

"Gee thanks, Art," Terry replied slowly. She thought about asking for her old job back. But her pride wouldn't permit it, even though she knew her money from the book wouldn't last long and there would be no more assignments from McMasters Publishing.

"Think nothing of it, dear," Art said expansively, hitching up his baggy trousers. "When your book comes out, you'll be in maybe to sign a few copies. I've already figured out where to put a big display. In this neighborhood, we'll sell hundreds. . . ."

"Gee, Art, I wouldn't get my hopes up too high," Terry warned, but Art waved her caution aside.

He pointed at the TV set on the counter. "I just saw your famous young man on the television announcing the marriage. Some big deal, huh?" he said, shaking his head in wonder.

Terry forced a smile to her lips that was as wan and tremulous as it could be, but Art continued on obliviously, "And he talked about the book, too. It's going to be a big, big success, I'm sure. . . ."

And once again Art beamed at her. Like some kindly old uncle, he put his arms out wide.

Terry quickly backed away, afraid that she was about to be the recipient of another hug and kiss. "Thanks again, Art, for the film and—and the faith. Bye."

Safely out on the street again, she walked briskly back to the house. She was preoccupied—melancholy thoughts and recollections mixing with her frantic planning for the end of her journey—so she barely noticed the old Chevy driving by.

Millie was behind the wheel, Terry could tell, *but who was that little balding man with her?*

The thought that he looked exactly like Caroll McMasters was just too ridiculous, and in the rush to finish getting ready it was easy to put the question of his identity out of her thoughts.

Within the hour, Terry was aboard a big jet at O'Hare. And by the time it was taxiing down the runway she had successfully pushed everything but the work still at hand from her mind. But her hard-won concentration was not to last.

chapter 10

It's amazing what you can accomplish when you set your mind to it and get organized, Terry thought to herself with some satisfaction as she repacked her camera bag and put it back into the trunk of her rented compact car.

Only an hour after leaving Chicago, she had disembarked at Epley Airport, just outside the bustling little metropolis of Omaha. She had picked up her waiting car, and a half an hour later she was taking pictures in Desoto, a wildlife refuge of nearly eight thousand acres that straddled both the Iowa and Nebraska banks of the Missouri River. At the center of the refuge was a calm, sparkling blue lake, created some years before—Terry learned from a visitor's brochure—by the U.S. Army Corps of Engineers from a horseshoe bend in the river.

As she wandered among the tourists and the picnickers, the fishermen and the boaters, she had found it impossible not to think of Brad and to wonder when he had last visited the refuge and what it would be like if they had come to this place together under happier circumstances.

As she had taken pictures of the lake—its waters dotted with swimmers, waterskiers and powerboaters, all come to escape the unseasonable heat—she imagined Brad cannonballing into the lake and in her mind's eye saw his strong, firm body cutting through the shimmering water.

Later, just before sunset, when she had taken her last photos of the day—of a proud angler in hip boots showing the day's catch to his beaming wife—she smiled to herself at the thought of how these simple people would have reacted if the famous Bradford Andrews had been there, standing close by her side.

But these speculations were fruitless, Terry knew; and as she slammed the trunk of the car she vowed to shut her mind to any more thoughts of the happiness and the ecstasy she could feel with Brad.

She got behind the wheel of the car and began her long drive west, heading directly into the brilliant, blazing sunset. Gradually it faded, its fiery reds and glowing oranges giving way to the same washed-out, gravid green that she and Brad had seen in southern Illinois one interminable day before.

How much had changed in one short day! Terry mused with a sigh, in spite of herself. Now all she wanted to do was to drive through the night to her last destination, the Sand Hills country of northwestern Nebraska. When she was done, she thought forlornly, there would be plenty of time to feel sad and miserable. Only when she had finally finished this assignment—she realized—would she be truly free of thoughts of Brad, and their time together, and of a happiness that was not meant to be.

The glowing green sky, lighted by the last rays of the setting sun, became streaked with amethyst, then turned ever deepening shades of blue—from turquoise to mulberry to sapphire—until finally night descended and the sky was black velvet sprinkled with bright stars.

By driving across the Great Plains at night, Terry was spared the sight of those endless flat expanses that many other drivers found so much less than inspiring. But even at night she sensed the wide vistas, the distant horizons, the immense skies. And as she drove on through the dark night, going ever west even as she edged north, the flat land became rugged.

In this most western part of the heartland, she left the plains behind and entered an endless land of bare ridges, sandy dunes, and grassy hills. This was farm country no longer; this was a land of vast ranches, and the main crop was cattle not grain.

For company as she drove Terry turned on the car radio. But as luck would have it she tuned right into the entertainment news:

"*. . . and Brad Andrews is making news again. The network-news superstar . . .*"

Click. Terry couldn't bear to listen to the announcement of Brad's wedding, or anything else that he was up to for that matter. As she switched stations a light rain began to fall.

"*. . . we'll be back to mellow music in just a few seconds, but first some weather. We got good news for the farmers tonight! That front stalled over the Rockies for the last couple of days is beginning to move, and we've got cool, dry air coming down from Canada to push out that mass of damp, sticky marine air from the Gulf that's been giving us all the miseries and the prickly heat the last couple of days. And that means rain, folks, lots of it! There's a flash-flood watch on for parts of Colorado, Wyoming, and western Nebraska, and the Weather Service is reporting funnel clouds sighted in . . .*"

Click. Terry turned off the radio, switched on her windshield wipers and concentrated on driving on the narrow, winding asphalt highway made slick by the misty rain. Like the raindrops that came out of nowhere to pelt her window, thoughts of Brad kept flying to the surface of her mind.

She remembered how he had predicted the gathering storm, and the pleasure he took in the bits of lore passed on to him by his father and grandfather. . . . She could hear him once again telling the Indian legend of the saw-whet and, suddenly, could practically feel him edging closer to her, unable to contain his rising passion. . . . In the falling rain, she could once again smell the sea, hear the waves crashing on the lake shore, feel the heat of Brad's touch. . . .

No! Terry pounded the steering wheel with one hand. She took a deep breath and shook her head from side to side, as if she could shake the very thoughts from her mind. She turned the radio on again, dialing past the all-news station, the country music station with its songs of unrequited love, the rock music station filling the airwaves with pulsating teenage lust, until she finally found the nondescript instrumental "pop music" she was looking for.

The rain stopped. She turned off the wipers and relaxed a bit. For a time she hummed along to the dance music that filled the car. Then she turned that off, too, rolled her window down and listened to the sybillant hiss of the humid air as it rushed past the open car window.

The time went by. And at last, after midnight, Terry arrived at her final destination.

The toothless, white-bearded old codger in the long nightshirt, standing on the other side of the big ranch house's screen door, could have been Gabby Hays's twin brother. Not only his appearance, but his crusty voice and his curmudgeon-like attitude reminded Terry of the old actor who had played the feisty sidekick to a thousand cowboy heroes in the fondly remembered Saturday morning television of her youth.

She just had to smile back at him even though it wasn't exactly good news or Western hospitality that he was extending to her.

"I tell you, lady, we're not open," he said, in a voice cracking with impatience. "For the third time, I don't care how late it is, I don't care if you've got cash or even gold. And if you think you can influence old Ernest Cobb with that pearly-white smile of yours, or jest because you're purttier than a mountain sunrise, well Missy, the answer is still *NO!*"

Before he could slam the door in her face, Terry

quickly asked, "But this is the Bar D Ranch, isn't it, Mister Cobb?"

"Yep," the old man allowed suspiciously.

"And this is a dude ranch?" Terry continued. "You do take visitors, you do accommodate the public?"

Obviously offended, Ernest Cobb drew himself up to his full five-and-a-half-foot height. "The Bar D is *not* a dude ranch. For your information, Missy, there are *no* dude ranches in the Sand Hills. The Bar D is a working cattle ranch. . . . We do sometimes accommodate the public, it's true," he admitted. "You might even say we have resort facilities, too, but we are definitely *not* a dude ranch."

"Oh . . . I see, Mr. Cobb," Terry replied, trying to seem reasonable. "I don't mean to offend you, and I do realize that I've come very late at night, but can't you put me up for just one night? That's all I want."

"It's what I been tryin' to tell you, Missy," Cobb said. "We're all booked up, all our accommodations is sold, ever' last one."

Terry persisted. "You're booked up, so early in the season? Surely, that's not possible."

Cobb was growing more exasperated. "Goldarn, I'm tellin' ya this big Eastern fellah booked the whole shebang, ever' last room! Said he wanted it to himself 'fore the season started. Said he didn't rightly know jest when he was gonna get here, but that don' matter none 'cause the whole dang place's his for the week. He paid for it, understand?"

Terry did, indeed, understand. The light was beginning to dawn. "This 'big Eastern fellah' of yours, he wouldn't be a TV newscaster, would he?"

The old man scratched his scraggly beard. "Well,"

he said after a moment's reflection. "I don' like to watch the television out here, don' get a very good picture anyhow, but I do believe that's so. He is some sort of TV fellah, now that you mention it."

"And would his name be Bradford Andrews?"

"Why, yes it would," Cobb said, shaking his head up and down. "That's his name all right. I remember; I don' even have to look it up in the ledger."

"Well, that settles it then," Terry said firmly. "I'm with the Andrews party. I just came ahead, that's all."

"'Came ahead,' is it?" Cobb repeated suspiciously. "Jest a second, Missy."

He disappeared from the open doorway for a few seconds, then came back clutching a big, black leather ledger book in his arms.

Peering into it, he asked, "Would you be T. Rew-vack?"

Terry smiled. "Terry Rovik," she said, correcting him graciously. She took out her wallet from her shoulder bag and showed him her license.

The old man studied it carefully, then handed the license back to her. "Well, gol-*lee,* why didn't you say so in the first place?"

Terry could hardly keep from thinking about Brad with each and every waking thought, no matter how hard she willed herself not to, so keeping him out of her dreams proved to be impossible. It was a sultry night, and anything more than fitful sleep in the soft brass bed was hopeless.

As she tossed and turned and moaned in her sleep, she could *see* once again his muscular torso and strong hands, the veins of his neck and arms pulsing and prominent as he knelt beside her, kneading her soft skin; she could *feel* the feverish, moist touch of his lips as he covered her face with kisses; she could *hear* the passion and urgency of his whispered endearments; she could *taste* the saltiness of his skin; she could *smell* his manly scent as it mingled with the pungent aroma of the lake shore, wafting in on a cool sea breeze. . . .

She awoke with a start, just after dawn. The big ranch house, surrounded by cottonwoods and elder trees, was at the top of a high ridge overlooking a broad, grassy valley, and the small, cozy room old Cobb had given her was at the top of the ranch house, just under the front eaves.

Terry hopped out of the downy brass bed and threw open the west window, which gave her a spectacular view of the ranch operations and the Sand Hills country all around. The air was still hot and muggy, but a hint of a fresh breeze was blowing in. Although the sky above the ranch house was a brilliant, early morning blue, a line of massive, angry, black clouds was already beginning to boil up over the distant horizon.

Quickly, Terry washed her face at the little sink just under the window. The dramatic early morning light, casting long shadows into the valley, was perfect, so she pulled out her cameras and began shooting through the window.

She took pictures of the large, saddle-roofed barn, of the corrals, the pens, and the chutes for running cattle. She snapped the flagpole in front of the main house, topped by an American flag waving in the morning breeze, and, nearby, three skeletal white towers, at the pinnacles of which were rotating, steel gray windmills. She used a telephoto lens for shots of the several cowboys in boots, faded jeans and ten-gallon hats, who came swaggering out of a little bunkhouse, mounted horses, or got into battered pickups and headed out for their morning chores.

From her rooftop vantage point, she was also able to get photos of antelope and mule deer ranging along the distant grass-covered sand dunes of the wild country all around the ranch buildings. She snapped horses and cows, wild geese and ducks, ring-necked pheasants flapping out from the cover of brown thickets. . . .

And then, with the early morning sun glinting from its wingtips, a little silver airplane that she had come to know so well appeared in the sky above, banked high over the valley, then turned and buzzed the ranch house. Off in the distance, lightning flashed in the approaching storm bank and the wind began to rise.

With eyes wide and her hand at her mouth, Terry watched the plane circle again and come in low on the ranch's dirt airstrip, about a quarter of a mile away, on the floor of the valley.

Heart pounding uncontrollably, she looked on from her high window as old Ernest Cobb came riding out from the barn on a black mare, holding in one hand the reins of a second horse—a spirited palomino—that he led at a fast trot down to the waiting Beechcraft.

She saw Brad—wearing a blue satin jacket with red piping on the arms, the sun reflecting from his mirrored aviator sunglasses—hop down from the aircraft to an enthusiastic greeting from Mr. Cobb. With easy grace he mounted the palomino and galloped toward the ranch house.

By the time Cobb led Brad into the big, beam-ceilinged living room, Terry was waiting there, a red print Western shirt tucked into her tight white shorts, the sockless white tennis shoes emphasizing her long brown legs. She was standing on the far side of the room, her hands held demurely at her sides.

Old Cobb blathered on, oblivious to how they looked at each other: ". . . 25,000 acres with fine hunting and fishing, miles and miles of riding trails and all the peace and quiet you . . ."

"Hi, Brad," Terry whispered in a soft voice barely audible across the room. Again, the past was forgotten; only sheer will power kept her from running to him and throwing herself in his arms.

"Terry." He pulled off the sunglasses, saying her name as if it were a magical word. "I—I was afraid you wouldn't be here, that I wouldn't see you again. . . ."

Old Cobb stopped abruptly in the center of the room, midway between Terry and Brad. He looked from one to the other, but neither one looked back at him. "Landsakes, children, but I do believe I'll leave you two alone for jest a minute. I'll be in the kitchen back there, whippin' up some cakes an' eggs an' a pot a hot coffee. Come on back when yer ready," he added in his creaky voice as he hurried off, an embarrassed half-smile playing across his grizzled face.

"I—I'm glad to see you," Terry admitted in a small voice choked with emotion. "I—I didn't think I would be after I left you back in that hotel bar, after all—after all that's happened, but I am. . . ."

"Terry." Again he said her name as if it were an incantation. Then, like a stallion breaking from the starting gate, he moved across the room. Five long strides carried him to her. She put a hand up as if to resist, but he swept her into his arms and pulled her close to him.

"Terry, Terry, there's so much to say, so much to explain to you. . . . I hardly know where to begin." He bent toward her upturned face, his lips brushed hers.

"No!" Terry gasped, pulling away. "I want to, I swear, but I can't."

For a second they stood facing each other, looking deeply into each other's eyes. In the silence, Terry became aware of the rain that was now beating steadily against the windows of the ranch house. Outside the wind was still rising.

"You know, you're right," Brad said at last. He took her by the hand and led her gently toward the front door. "Let's go outside on the porch, listen to the rain, and watch the storm—it used to be one of my favorite pastimes when I was a kid. We can talk," he added softly. "There's a lot to explain."

Outside, from the shelter of the covered porch, they stood side by side holding hands, like two awe-struck children looking out over the little valley as the sky above them turned dark as dusk and the huge thunderstorm hit.

The rain came down in sheets.

Lightning flashed.

The thunder cracked.

Like an approaching freight train, the wind howled.

"You know, you messed up all my plans," Brad mused, so quietly that Terry had to strain to hear over the savage thunderstorm. He laughed to himself. "I had good news for us, a present—it was all arranged—then you hopped on that truck."

"What?" Terry asked, puzzled. "I don't understand."

"That trucker, I got him a job," Brad replied with a smile. "I found him another job. . . ."

"You what?"

A gust of wind sent rain splattering into the porch. Instinctively, they both stepped back a pace, and Brad put his arm around Terry's shoulder. "I was so devastated when you left me in that bar that I stayed for a couple of drinks, and then a couple more. The bartender told me what happened, how you were kind enough to talk with Big Jerry when he was down, feeling lonely and missing his woman," Brad explained.

"At that moment, it was a feeling that I could appreciate, in fact it was just how I was feeling myself. I made a point of calling New York that night. When he gets back to his wife, there'll be a letter waiting for him, offering him the position of driver for the network's Mid-South Mobile Unit. There's a lot of expensive equipment on a big truck, and the network can use a reliable man to drive it. The pay's twice as much, and he'll never be away from his wife for more than a day at a time. . . ."

Terry was flabbergasted. "But why?"

"I wanted a way to make it up to you. I was happy, I had a new job myself, I wanted everybody in the world to be as happy as I was. Hell, I'm even thinking of calling Rick, that kid who was our chauffeur in Minneapolis, and making him my East Coast driver or assistant, or whatever it is that *he* wants. . . ."

"A *new job,* you say you have a new job. . . ."

Brad's revelations were coming as fast as the lightning bolts that flashed all around them and the torrents of rain descending from the dark heavens. Terry was nonplussed: what would he say next?

"Uh-huh, a new job. Here, look at this." From the pocket of his satin jacket Brad took a crumpled slick newspaper with the word VARIETY written in bold green script across the top. "Read the lead story on the front page."

With difficulty, Terry tore her gaze from Brad and looked down at the newspaper headline, which read: MOORHOUSE NAMED NETWORK PREXY, and the sub-headline below it, which added: *"Andrews Tapped As News Division Chief."*

Terry quickly scanned the first few paragraphs of the story:

". . . Minneapolis affiliate manager Martin A. Moorhouse, named network president by the ConAm board, today reached through the network corporate ranks to make Bradford Andrews, well-known TV news glamour boy, the youngest-ever head of a major network news division.

"'We need someone at the top who the public trusts, someone of proven news judgment and absolute personal probity, and Brad Andrews is that man,' Moorhouse said in a statement released today, thus ending months of insider speculation . . ."

"Oh, Brad, that's wonderful!" Terry said enthusiastically, looking up at him. The wind whistled harder, driving the rain sideways; like cosmic strobe lights, like the fireworks on the Fourth of July, the lightning cracked and flashed. Terry shouted to make herself heard above the roaring wind and thunder.

"Is *this* why you had to rush back to New York that night in the Paradise Lodge? Is *this* what you couldn't talk about?"

"I wanted to tell you then—but I just couldn't," he answered.

"Oh, Brad," Terry asked fearfully, thinking of Caroline McMasters, "what are we going to do? What's going to happen to us?"

"Maybe we're finally going to get lucky. . . . Terry?"

"Yes?"

Brad reached into his jacket pocket. "There's something I want you to see." From his right-hand pocket he pulled a rectangular case, just slightly larger than the size of a cigarette pack.

"What is it?" Terry asked curiously.

"It's a video cassette of a talk show I did as a favor for an old friend a few days ago when I was in New York. I brought it because when you look at that tape you're going to find out something. . . ."

"Find out what?" Terry asked as the rain came down in sheets.

"That I didn't announce my marriage to Caroline McMasters on that show," Brad said, gazing into her eyes.

"You didn't? But I *heard* you—or rather, I *thought* that's what you said. But—but how did you know that's what I thought, I mean . . ."

"I'm a reporter," Brad replied in a clipped voice. "When my mother got back from California the first thing she did was send me an urgent message in Chicago to tell me about her visit with you. It was only then that, *finally,* I realized what was going on!" I forced my way into your house to explain to you, but by then you were already taking off from O'Hare.

"But Millie was there!" Brad said in a loud voice. The lightning flashed and the thunder cracked. "Good old Millie had taken action, too! She had just returned from a meeting with Caroll McMasters. . . ."

Terry was shocked. "I *did* see them together," she said to herself. Outside the lightning flashed, illuminating the little porch with the intensity of a gigantic strobe light.

A whirling blast of wind whistled past them.

In a determined voice Brad continued: "Caroll's a decent fellow and Sarah's ruse made him feel terrible. He admitted all to Millie right away. . . ."

"Sarah's *ruse?*" Terry whispered, her voice lost in the noise of the storm.

"Sarah's been determined that I should marry her daughter Caroline from the first day we met. When *I* insisted that *you*—an unknown—be the photographer for the book I was going to do for them . . ."

"*You* insisted?"

For just a split second, Brad grinned impishly at her. "That's right. I knew how you felt about me—after I deserted you. I knew from my mother's spies how you could have your pick of eligible men. I had to have *some way* to get back together with you again. Besides, I couldn't have found a better photographer, even Sarah admitted that. But when she took one look at you, during that first meeting you had with her and Caroll, she realized on the spot that you spelled trouble for her grand plan to get me together with Caroline. That's why she got you to make that promise to her, that's why she played on your decent impulses. Oh, I suppose in a way her attitude is understandable, but still . . ."

"You mean—" Terry began, but a tremendous clap

of thunder shook the porch and drowned out her words.

"Just so!" Brad shouted triumphantly. "I never intended to marry Caroline McMasters! *Never!* She's an old friend, that's all. . . ."

Terry was flabbergasted. "But—but Sarah said you two . . . in Europe . . ."

"Oh, we saw each other in Europe all right. I helped her elope with this Italian count she fell for—a good chap, but utterly penniless. Naturally, poor Caroline was terrified to tell her mother. . . ."

Terry's confusion persisted. Her thoughts whirled like the storm clouds above. The pandemonium in her mind matched the chaos of the turbulent tempest. "But the note . . . the one you found in your pocket at the lodge . . . the one that sent you racing back to New York . . ."

The thunder boomed. "You mean the one from Carruthers?" Brad shouted. "He's my best line producer. He told me the corporation's Board had ordered me back to New York for a top-secret meeting. It had nothing at all to do with Caroline. . . ."

With a realization as sudden as one of the lightning flashes outside, Terry remembered her second meeting with the McMasters family and, in her mind's eye, again saw Caroline go to make a long-distance phone call: it was the Italian count she was calling, not Brad! Terry smiled with delight. Was the storm ending, or did she imagine it? Would the sun once again shine down on her—and Brad?

"As soon as Millie told me about Caroll's confession, I knew I had to find you quickly," Brad yelled above the distant thunder. "I tracked you to the art gallery—Damien told me about your reaction to the talk show—then I went to the photo store where you used to work and Art told me how you ran out when he tried to congratulate you on our engagement. . . ."

"*Our* engagement?!" Could she have heard him right through the noise of the fading but still potent storm?

Brad reached into his other pocket. "Here," was all he said.

Gingerly, Terry took the tiny leather-covered box from his hand.

"Open it, Terry," Brad said gruffly. "Open it now."

She opened the little box. Inside, on red velvet, sparkled the biggest diamond ring she had ever seen in her entire life; its facets blazed with a fire that outshone even the lightning. Next to the ring was a simple gold chain.

Terry held the ring up. "Oh Brad . . ."

"I was planning to give it to you at the Paradise Lodge," Brad shouted above the wind, "but it didn't work out the way I expected. . . ."

Terry picked up the shining chain, from which hung a greenstone, the very color of the stormy air. She remembered the afternoon on the Lake Superior shore, walking ahead of their horses, when she had picked up this stone and handed it to him. "Oh Brad," she repeated.

"I had the necklace made as a memento of the wonderful time that we had," Brad explained, "and to try to make it up to you for how it ended."

"Darling," Terry began, wanting to tell him everything was all right, that this was the happiest moment of her life. Tears of joy came to her eyes as Brad took her in his arms.

"Terry . . . one more thing . . ."

"What, Brad?"

"Marry me, Terry."

The lightning flashed far away, but Terry hardly noticed it. She smiled radiantly, a smile that seemed to part the very clouds. "Of course I will, darling," she said, turning her face up to his.

Brad kissed her, with an intensity that rivaled the very height of the electrical storm. Terry wanted the kiss—and the moment—to last forever. As their lips finally parted, so did the last of the clouds.

All around them were brilliant streamers of morning light. To Terry it seemed the sheer force of her happiness had dispersed the storm.

After the storm finally spent itself over the trackless, unpopulated dunes, everything looked fresh and green and cool. While Brad was in the kitchen talking to Cobb, Terry took the talk-show videotape into a small back office of the well-equipped ranch house where there was a color television hooked up to a Betamax video recorder. There, with ever-increasing happiness and an ever-widening smile, she sat watching the show unfold.

She listened as the talk-show host and Brad exchanged pleasantries and reminiscences of their days as young reporters together.

She listened as they talked together of the book that Brad was doing—*their* book—and as the host convinced Brad to reveal a confidence.

"Are you going to tell our viewers why you look so happy?" the talk-show host prompted.

"Okay, Mike, just for old times, and because this show isn't aired until later this week and you've promised to keep my secret until then . . ."

And then Brad revealed that he was going to ask the young woman who was working as the photographer on the book to marry him.

"Marriage, is it?" the talk-show host asked genially.

"Yes," Brad replied emphatically, *"marriage."*

Terry smiled to herself as the studio audience oohed and aahed.

She smiled again as the talk-show host explained that they didn't have a photo of the lucky young lady but would show instead a group photograph of the husband and wife publishing team that was producing Brad's book. Included in the picture was their beautiful young daughter, Caroline.

"Well, all I can say," joked the talk-show host, "is what a stunner your fiancée must be, Brad, if this was the girl you passed up." Terry shared the audience's good-natured laughter.

A grin lingered on her face as she switched off the video recorder and wandered outside to the flower-filled meadow behind the ranch house. She was lost in happy thought, breathing in the cool fresh air when Brad joined her.

"Old Ernest Cobb's going to be cooking for us," he said, "while we catch up on lost time—upstairs in our room. I've arranged for him to bring all our meals there, just like years ago, back at the Paradise Lodge."

"Brad, it's wonderful," Terry whispered, coming close to him. Touching his arm lightly, she stood on tiptoe and kissed him. "I was such a fool," she admitted with a wry smile. "I just finished looking at that tape. Now I know. . . ."

Warmly, Brad smiled back at her. "Well, that takes

care of just about everything," he said with some satisfaction. "There's just one more thing . . ."

"Oh?"

". . . my proposal, you do accept it? You're certain?"

"Your proposal," Terry repeated coquettishly. "Just what proposal might that be, Mr. Andrews?"

Brad took her in his arms. His smile was full of love. "Oh, let's see. . . . First of all, I'm proposing to be the first news-division head in history to remain a working reporter."

"Is that so?" Terry arched an eyebrow and Brad lightly kissed it.

"And," he continued, "I'm proposing to give *you* a video camera. With that sharp eye of yours, in no time at all you are going to be the *best* cameraperson a working reporter ever had. *And* . . ."

"Those are good ones," Terry said, snuggling up closer in Brad's arms. "Got any other proposals?" she prompted with a pixieish smile.

Brad kissed the tip of her nose. "Just one more," he said, looking straight into her eyes. "I want you to be my wife."

Terry held up her hand and wiggled the fingers. There, on her finger, sparkled the diamond ring.

"Oh yes," she said. "Oh yes, oh yes."

As they embraced and kissed in the glistening field beneath a brilliant blue sky, Terry felt she had come home at last. She had traveled through America's heartland and found her heart's desire.